# LORD

## Of The

# WILDS

## By

## Rita Hesmond

Copyright © 2021 Rita Tremain

Lord of the Wilds

**ISBN-13** 979-8543008461

**Publisher** Independently published

Cover design: H Jaeschke from a photograph by Peter Tremain

# Contents

# Chapter 1

"Is this all there is then?" Marie was feeling restless.

She shoved a cushion up against the arm of the sofa and turned to face Henry. She wanted a discussion, a chance to review where they were at in their lives, but seeing that he was tired, she softened.
Friday evening was probably not the best time for a serious conversation, but the kids were in bed and for once they were not zoned out watching Netflix.

"I'm not trying to get at you," she said, pushing a stray curl behind her ear, "But we're ticking all the boxes and it's still not really satisfying is it? Don't you feel the same?"

"I know work is pretty meaningless," Henry brought his feet down off the coffee table and crossed his long legs. She'd gained his attention now. "But that's modern life isn't it, for most people, you sell a third of your time in exchange for the means to live. If you're lucky there's a bit extra for the things you really enjoy, a few luxuries maybe and a holiday. I guess it's different if you're creative, an artist or something, but most of us are either making widgets or marketing the widgets or financing the widgets. It is pretty crazy, put like that." He smiled, the beginning of lines crinkling round his eyes, white teeth. "I don't know how we got here."

"Well I can answer that one," she laughed, "you wouldn't leave me alone, remember, bombarding me with texts, calling all the time, you turned up with roses!"

Marie had been living in a house share after uni and Henry came round with a friend. There had been instant chemistry; she liked his height, his thick dark hair and the warmth in his eyes. She only came up to his shoulder, she moved like a dancer, and he thought her skin was golden. He was soon enchanted. She had nearly gone home that weekend which could have altered the whole course of their lives. On the other hand, she quite liked to think, they were destined to meet and fall in love, though whether the mortgage and juggling work with the school run were part of the celestial plan she wasn't so sure.

"Do you ever wonder what it would be like if we didn't live in the city?" she asked him.

"The work is here," he said, "and I can't see us living in some random county town can you? I know we could get a better house further out but it's boring in the 'burbs', we've always said so. And we'd spend more time commuting."

"I'm not thinking of a bigger house," Marie said, " but a different existence altogether. I don't know what, but somewhere with fresh air and countryside and, I don't know, a way of life not just a job."

"That's a bit radical isn't it?" he countered, " Like those programmes where people buy a French chateau and do weddings or make wine?"

"That sounds glamorous but the reality is it would be more hard work and stress, and anyway we don't speak the language, " Marie replied. " I just don't want to waste our whole lives on a treadmill like your grand parents. They had to wait until they retired to move to Exmoor."

He got up, asking "Do you want another drink?"

"Go on then, if you like."

Marie's gaze followed his slim, athletic figure as he crossed through the dining room and into the open plan extension they had designed a few years before. She considered the comfortable home they had created with its mixture of modern and slightly bohemian décor which was her own particular style. Now, lulled by the cosy fire Henry had lit in the black wrought iron fireplace, and her candles burning on the hearth, she told herself,

'Really, I should be satisfied with my life just as it is,' feeling a twinge of guilt at her ingratitude.

Henry came back with a bottle of Montepulciano and refilled their glasses. While he was in the kitchen he had been thinking, and told her,

"I remember those times on Exmoor, when I stayed with my grand parents in the summer holidays. There was a farming family who had sheep and cows. I got to know the sons and one year I helped out with the hay making. That all seemed pretty idyllic in those days; I used to envy Thomas and Josh. I never wanted to go back home, though I expect it was hard work running that farm. There was always something on, shearing, hedging and ditching, that sort of thing. They were lucky I suppose, you have to be born to that way of life. I expect they're still at it."

"It does sound wonderful to be so close to nature, to be part of it," Marie sounded wistful. Henry drew her bare feet across his lap, kneading her toes.

"I can see you in a long white floaty dress with a crook in your hand, you'd make a good shepherdess," he teased. His large hands gliding up the smooth skin under

7

her skirt brought an end to the conversation, but it had sown a seed in both of them.

Marie was worried about her friend Sally who was in a difficult relationship, so the following morning she went round for a coffee while Jack was at football practice and Chloe had her ballet class. There was a moment of irritation as she pulled out of their gate; someone had parked too close again and she had to do a three point turn just to avoid the cars parked opposite. It didn't help that already traffic was waiting and the driver of a white van was hanging out of his window trying to hurry her up.

'This is ridiculous,' she thought, 'Everyone else seems to have two cars these days.'

Saturday traffic was building up as she queued to get onto the main road and Marie hoped she wouldn't be held up for too long.

She knew Matthew would be out so things weren't likely to turn awkward as long as he didn't come back early. Sally's partner was controlling; he discouraged her from seeing friends and if she was out he found excuses to call and check up on her. Marie couldn't see herself getting into that sort of relationship, let alone putting up with it, but part of the smothering was unexpected treats and presents and lavish praise if Sally's behaviour 'improved' as he put it. There were mixed messages going on and Sally seemed to have lost the ability to see her situation clearly.

Marie was glad to see that the parking space outside the flat was empty, and the door opened as soon as she rang the bell. Sally had obviously been looking out for her.

8

Marie's innocuous greeting, "Hello, how are you ?" seemed to have become a loaded question question however. Sally was defensive, and quick to brush off even this standard enquiry.

"I'm fine, why wouldn't I be?" and then hugged Marie impulsively to dispel the sudden awkwardness.

"What have you been up to anyway?" she asked brightly.

Marie thought Sally looked anything but fine, she was pale and there were shadows under her eyes.
She didn't comment though and instead started telling her news, and confided about her growing restlessness.

"I can't put my finger on it, it's as if the wind has changed and I feel something is coming."

Sally suggested she do a tarot reading; she was good at interpreting the cards, and was pleased to deflect attention away from herself.

"You'll need to ask a specific question," Sally said as she shuffled the traditional Rider Waite pack, "You need to be clear in your own mind exactly what you want to know."

"OK," Marie was struggling to come up with the words. "Are we going to change our way of life ?"

" Let's see," said Sally, as she laid out the cards. As Marie's hand hovered over the backs of the cards, she immediately felt drawn to choose and turned over the Ace of Pentacles.

"That whole suit is concerned with the earth, which may be the realm of nature itself, but also worldly matters like your finances, career, things like that. Since you have picked the Ace which concerns potential," Sally explained as she handed the card to Marie, "we're

9

talking about your future situation."

When Marie drew The Tower card next, the image seemed negative to her, but Sally said,

"The Tower falling is the old familiar situation crumbling, again it's a card associated with the earth and nature, down to earth you might say in the sense of agriculture and financial ventures."

Marie couldn't think of any big financial ventures they were likely to undertake, but when she drew the Queen of Pentacles, the image seemed to have more understandable associations.

"A woman surrounded by nature, in her element and in a nurturing role."

Marie felt that fitted her personality quite well, she did love nature and as a wife and mother she was happy to nurture others, so long as she had some time to pursue her own interests.

As Marie thanked Sally for the reading, she became aware that her friend was now on edge; she was nervous in case Matthew came home and found she had company. Sensing the reason for her unease, Marie stood up to go, but she couldn't resist asking whether Sally had seen any of their mutual friends, did she know Jane was pregnant? No, Sally hadn't heard.

"I've been really busy with work," she said, "but that's great news, I'll give her a call."

"What about your mother, wasn't she going to come for a visit?"

"Oh we've put that off for a bit," Sally was opening the door.

Going down the stairs, Marie reflected that Sally wouldn't welcome her mother's advice right now, any more than she wanted her friends' opinions. Sally knew what everyone would say but either she thought she was sorting things out for herself, or more worryingly, she was just frozen like a rabbit in the headlights. Either way, it gave Marie the shivers.

'And we didn't even get round to a coffee,' she realised.

Still, as she went off to round up her children, Marie was encouraged to think that the reading chimed with the theme she and Henry had begun to explore the previous evening.

That afternoon the family went round to their allotment, although in the winter there was only tidying to do. There were a few sprouts and cabbages left and Henry collected some potatoes he had been storing in the shed. They had waited a long time for their name to come up on the list and Henry had wanted to put up a poly tunnel but that was against the rules. He wanted to grow melons and peppers and the small greenhouse in their garden wasn't big enough to do more than experiment with a few varieties. There was a community garden adjoining the allotments and every weekend families met up there, so there was always someone for the children to play with.

Seeing Jack's curly brown head emerging from the higher branches of the one large tree and Chloe hanging upside down from the railing, her long hair trailing on the path, Marie thought, 'My feral kids need more space and room to grow.'

Chloe and Jack were desperate for a dog, patting every one they met in the park, asking their names and age, running back to their parents pleading and promising "We'll look after it!"

At last the day came when Henry and Marie gave in, after a serious discussion about the practicalities. The two cats, Samson and Delilah were no trouble, they used the cat flap and were fairly self-sufficient. A dog would be a much bigger responsibility of course.

Henry worked for a firm of management consultants and was in the office all day, or visiting clients, but Marie worked for the city education department organising inset training days and continuing professional development courses for teachers, which involved a lot of site visits and she organised her own time. At a push she could pop back home at lunchtimes most days and her parents lived close by, which was one reason for living in that area. They were willing to help with childcare, and that would now occasionally have to include dog minding as well.

The children were jumping about with excitement when the family arrived at the rescue centre and had to be told to be quiet before they went in. It was the same shelter where they had adopted the cats, so when they called, the receptionist had waived the usual home visit. They told the volunteer who showed them around that they were looking for an adult dog from one of the easy breeds, a Shihtzu cross or a West Highland terrier perhaps, but they came out with a half-grown collie bitch for no better reason than that she stood on her hind legs against the bars and beseeched them with her big brown eyes .

Henry and Marie were standing by an outside enclosure, meeting a three year old dog with impeccable credentials, when Chloe and Jack ran round the corner at full pelt saying,

"You have to come and see this one, she looks so sad, she really, really needs a home. The lady says she's been here ages and nobody wants her."

Of course Henry and Marie had their reservations, as they were shown into an enclosed area by a senior staff member who left them in no doubt that this dog would be a bit of a challenge.

"I feel I have to warn you, if you haven't had a collie before, they're really working dogs. They need a lot of exercise and clear direction. I've no doubt this one has a heart of gold and hasn't a vicious bone in her body, but the only socialising she's had is with us, and we really don't have the time here to train a young dog."

Henry and Marie exchanged glances as the children ran round in circles with the collie, which had been brought in to join them.

"For Heaven's sake, calm down you two, she's excited enough as it is, being let out of her pen," Marie told them.

The children hunkered down and the dog lolloped up, licking their faces and putting her paws on their shoulders. None of them could face consigning her back to that sterile existence, so they signed the papers, made a generous donation  and led her out to the car.

They called her Taffy and it cost them a small fortune in chewed shoes and obedience classes before she settled down to being the ideal family dog,

"But we couldn't send her back there, could we?" they reminded each other in the early days, as they surveyed the carnage.

The addition of an active dog to exercise prompted expeditions further into the countryside outside the city and while Marie and Henry walked in the woods, Jack and Chloe climbed trees and built dens and Taffy got wet in streams.

The idea of getting out of the city hadn't gone away; it resurfaced regularly, especially when any problems arose at work. Henry's job was demanding and stressful. It was the partners who brought in the business, but he did much of the assessment and wrote up proposals and reports and it all seemed to be against a deadline since consultants were often only brought in when a crisis was looming. He confided his feelings to his father but got no sympathy.

"Any executive job has its pressures, that's what you're paid for," his father reminded him, "You got a good education and you should be on top of the game at your age. You need to get another promotion before you're forty, then you'll be better rewarded. Put yourself out there, do some networking. I don't think you're ambitious enough. Look at your sister, she's got her head screwed on."

As long as he could remember, Henry's older sister Margaret had been held up as an example. Her reputation as a barrister was growing and she had a flat overlooking the Thames, but with no partner or children Henry wondered sometimes if her life was as fulfilling as she made it seem. No doubt she had energy and drive but these days Henry was often reminded of Marie's question, 'Is this all there is?'

'I don't know why I bother telling Dad anything,'

Henry thought resentfully as he drove home, 'I never was enough like him and he's still trying to mould me in his image.'

Marie found her job unrewarding; teachers often felt they had enough to do without extra training, suspecting that the latest fashion in education would soon give way to the next new thing.

Over breakfast one Sunday morning, when the children had gone back upstairs, Marie shared her concerns.

"The Comprehensive has just had another abysmal Ofsted report and I dread the thought of sending Jack there in a couple of years. They've had two changes of principal, all the teachers who could retire early have gone and those who are left are either totally disillusioned or out of their depth. There's no discipline so they never get to grips with bullying and the governors try to play down that problem because they don't know how to tackle it. Mind you, I wouldn't want to be in their shoes, it's more than rebranding and a change of uniform can solve."

"And you don't think we can get him into St. Jude's?' Henry was only just beginning to take this on board.

"Not unless you want to become a Catholic. Lots of people have tried going to mass but they're not easily convinced you're sincere. Of course, they do take non-Catholics but we aren't in the catchment area so there's no hope. I don't suppose your parents..."

"Absolutely not," Henry was decisive. "They're not badly off but with interest rates the way they are, they haven't got the money these days for private education, and if they did it for Jack, what about Chloe in a few years time? And anyway, it'd only make us beholden to them."

Marie was aware that her in- laws thought Henry could have done better and that she wasn't sophisticated enough. In their world a wife should be a social asset, cultivating the right people and furthering her husband's glittering career. She certainly didn't want to be in their debt .They had to agree that there was no obvious solution, the kids were bright but not exactly scholarship material and even then there would be a large proportion of the fees to find.

# Chapter 2

It was a warm early Spring that year and Henry and Marie decided to take the children away for the half term break.

"What about the Lake District?" Marie suggested.

"Too far for just a week, too many hours driving for the kids, and anyway it'll be crowded," Henry objected.

"Yorkshire Dales?"

"The further North you go the colder it's going to be. Actually I'd like to go back to Exmoor, I haven't been since Grandad died. I'd like to go back to the village, and get a feel for the place again. Of course it might be a case of rose-tinted spectacles, but I'd like to see."

Marie knew very little about Exmoor, her family had usually headed straight on down to Cornwall, but one National Park was as good as another she supposed, so they started looking at self-catering accommodation online.

They were sitting at the kitchen table, each commenting on what they had found, when Henry said,

"That's amazing, it's the farm, I recognise it. Handy Cross! I'd forgotten what it was called. Looks as if they've gentrified it a bit, it's a lot tidier than I remember, but the house is the same. They're advertising two letting cottages, shall I call them?"

"Why not, go for it," Marie agreed. When Henry explained to the young woman who answered that he had known the family as a boy, she called,

"Thomas, an old friend of yours on the phone."

Henry suddenly felt embarrassed, perhaps he should just have enquired about the cottages and not tried to force an acquaintance, but as soon as he gave his name Thomas remembered him and seemed genuinely pleased.

"Oh I'm sorry, " he said, "Our cottages have been booked since last autumn, people tend to come back, you know? It's hard to get anything decent on the spur of the moment. Let me think. Ellie, did you say Josephine was letting her mother's place now she's gone into a home?"

The call ended with a promise to meet up while they were down and a fresh number to ring, which led to the offer of a comfortable cottage in the village.

The children packed and unpacked several times, with more toys than clothes finding their way into their bags until Marie intervened, but at last everything was stowed in their old Volvo estate, Taffy secured between the children's seats and the family set off for the West Country.

As they approached the village Henry at first thought that hardly anything had changed and  he took  pleasure in pointing out familiar landmarks to the family. Turning off the main road there was a large National Trust property which attracted droves of tourists who then came on into the main street where the nearest pub had been converted into a stylish hotel and restaurant.

" That's really changed," Henry told them. "It used to be quite rough but now there's that big extension on the side and a conservatory."

"Maybe we can have a meal there one evening," Marie suggested.

"If you like, but by the look of it, it'll be expensive. We'll have to see if they do anything the kids will eat."

Shops had changed hands of course; the greengrocers had become a cafe and there was a delicatessen as well as a shop selling art and decorative home wares, but the buildings were the same and Henry had no difficulty in finding the cottage which was at the quieter end of the street. Few tourists ventured beyond the church, where there was a bend in the road and it narrowed to a lane, eventually becoming a back way to a smaller hamlet. Most people used the car park at the top of the village and left the same way as they had come in.

The cottage was cosy and there was a welcome pack in the fridge, so the family were in high spirits as they set out to explore the village before it got dark. Marie was delighted as they wandered up the High Street.

"These buildings look really old, those thatched houses must be, what, sixteenth century?"

"I guess so," said Henry, surveying the scene anew with adult eyes." Look at those beams, and this one has a round bulge in the end wall under the chimney, I'm sure that must be a bread oven."

"That's incredible, " Marie was soaking up the atmosphere. " Imagine living with all that history, there's a real sense of continuity and belonging here."

They chose a table in the cafe at the window, where they ate delicious home made pizza and played at identifying locals from the tourists or 'grockles' as they were called.

"They must be 'grockles'," Marie laughed, pointing out a couple wearing matching Barbours, "And he's local, that's not fresh mud on his boots, and that hat looks as if it lives in the foot well of a landrover!"

"You can't judge people round here by how they dress or what car they drive," Henry told her. "I've seen landed gentry in worn old waxed jackets driving beaten up four by fours. On Exmoor you're judged by the house you live in."

"That counts us out then," Marie said thoughtfully, "Judging by the estate agents we passed, house prices here are almost what they are at home."

"It's a sought after area, not as bleak as Dartmoor or as remote as Cornwall," Henry told her.

"Pity you didn't hang on to your grand parents bungalow, it'd be worth a lot today."

"Benefit of hindsight," Henry agreed , "But it wasn't my choice, Margaret wanted her share. Anyway, we'd never have done the extension without that inheritance."

The following day the family explored the village further and then headed up onto the moorland behind. Henry had to admit that his memories of the area were hazy; as a boy he had spent most of his time at his grand parents' home or up at the farm, but they found their way down off the hill to the river valley where they saw Exmoor ponies and some Red Devon cattle grazing peacefully. The ponies still had their thick dark winter coats.

"Pure bred Exmoors have that light mealy coloured muzzle and what's called a 'toad eye'," Henry told them. "You see the dark line?"

"It looks like eyeliner," Marie joked. Jack and Chloe tried to approach the ponies but they kept out of reach, eventually trotting away over the coarse heather, still dry and brown after the winter.

"They're wild ponies," Marie told them.

"Doesn't anyone look after them?" Chloe was concerned.

"It depends whether they are on National Trust Land or just in the National Park; they look after them. The farmers bring them hay in a bad winter. They live in managed herds anyway, and they're rounded up every Spring to check them over and take some of the young ones to break in as children's ponies," Henry told them. "In the old days the farmers used to ride them round to check their stock and farm children rode them over the hill to school sometimes."

"I wish I could have one," Chloe said longingly.

"I don't think there's enough grass on our back lawn," Jack teased her.

"We can go to the Exmoor Pony Sanctuary though," Marie promised, "it's not too far from here, and you can see them close up and pat them. "

Chloe was satisfied with that and the children went off to explore while Taffy sniffed for rabbits. Henry and Marie lay back on the short springy grass and watched a buzzard circling lazily on the thermals rising from the hill opposite. They felt the silence seep into their bones and although it was not quite warm enough to peel off their jackets, they felt so relaxed they could easily have fallen asleep.

Marie had sent a friend request to Thomas's wife Ellie on Facebook and that evening she got her profile up to look at the photos. There was Thomas with his thatch of sandy hair standing by an enormous tractor with a wide grin on his face. She showed the screen to Henry.

"Is that how you remember him?" she asked.

"Well he's filled out a bit, he looks like a No. 6."

"A what?"

"Heavyweight in the rugby scrum."

"Oh right. Here's Ellie on a quad bike with one of their sons behind her. She's very blonde. And here she is again with the women's skittles team. She isn't smiling in any of these photos, that's a bit odd; maybe she's a bit reserved."

"It's only a catch up, we don't have to see them again," he told her.

"Oh sure. Is this Josh? He's nothing like his brother is he?"

"He takes after their mother I think," Henry glanced at the screen. Marie was looking more closely; dark hair, chiselled features, slighter built than Thomas, looking into the camera with an enigmatic look in his grey eyes. It wasn't often Marie fancied anyone; too much at stake. She shook it off, don't even go there.

"He's the good looking one anyway," she commented, getting up to put the iPad away.

"Maybe this lunch wasn't such a good idea after all," Henry was teasing her, acknowledging her interest, but Marie thought she caught a hint of insecurity in his expression. She reached up to him,

"There's only room for one tall dark handsome man in my life," she assured him.

"I'm glad to hear it," he said, pulling her close.

'It doesn't get much better than this,' she thought hazily, feeling him rise against her.

The next day was Sunday and they met Thomas and Ellie at the 'locals' pub opposite the church for lunch.

Henry and Marie arrived first and chose a table within sight of the door. They agreed it was just what a country pub should be, not too smart, with wood panelling and red curtains and upholstery which didn't quite match. The ceilings were low and it was dark inside after the bright spring sunshine, but wall lights with their yellowing glass shades gave the place a homely feel. There was a polished wooden bar with stools where several older men were drinking Exmoor Ale from their own tankards kept on a shelf above the optics, a tradition already fast dying out. Meeting up for a pint before going home to their wives for Sunday dinner was a time honoured ritual not in decline, however.

The pub's carvery with a choice of several meats,was laid out on a long table in the dining room next door and the smell was making them hungry so the children were clamouring to eat .

Fortunately, it was not long before Thomas and Ellie came in with their two sons who were a bit older than Jack, followed by Thomas's younger brother Josh, and Henry got up to shake hands, introducing his family and then going to the bar to order a round. Soon they were all seated at a large table in the dining room tucking into plates piled high with meat, roast potatoes, gravy and yorkshire puddings, in the boys' case hardly leaving room for any vegetables.

"Well, this is nice!" Thomas said expansively, looking around the table with satisfaction. "It was really good to hear from you. So what have you been doing all these years, apart from getting yourself hitched to this lovely lady of course?"

He smiled  broadly at Ellie and she took his attempt at

gallantry  as it was intended and smiled back. Henry gave them a short- hand version of his life to date, playing down anything that might make him sound too much like a city executive.

"But what about you?" he asked, including Josh in his enquiry. "From the website it looked like you are running the farm now?"

"Dad died of a heart attack ,what, eight years ago," Thomas told them. "That was a shock, it was very sudden. Of course he never would take care of himself, worked all hours, ate too many fry ups. He used to talk about indigestion but we wonder now if he was getting heart pain all along and was ignoring it. After that we just carried on, as you do. We had started converting the old cottages for holiday accommodation so there was a lot to do, and Josh is converting the big barn into a house for himself."

"Do you not need the barn for the farm now then?" Henry was curious.

"Oh you're better off with modern agricultural buildings these days, much more practical. And there are grants to diversify if you know how to apply for them." Thomas told them  their mother had remarried, and the brothers owned their farm, so it was all a good investment Henry realised, lucky for them.

There was a lot to catch up on and Thomas did most of the talking. Henry remembered that Josh had always been the quieter of the two brothers.  The children got tired of all the talk and Josh told them,

" You can play snooker next door if no-one else wants the table, but don't tear  the baize for Heaven's sake."

The boys went off but Chloe was shy and leaned on

her mother's shoulder. Marie put her arm round her.

"Don't you want to go and play with the boys darling?"

Chloe shook her head and stayed securely where she was. Ellie and Marie started comparing notes about schools and Marie was interested to hear that the secondary school in town had a good reputation. Neither of Ellie's boys was academic but they were doing well enough and plenty of local children, particularly the girls, went on to good universities.

Thomas was telling them how expensive life had become for farmers and how difficult it was to make a good living from the land. A lot of the farms were leasehold, which usually got handed down through the generations, though often it wasn't easy to find the rent on quarter day. Later they could not remember how Holtbourne was first mentioned. The holding was up for sale; the house came with only 60 acres, so by any standards it was really too small to support a family as anyone with any experience would know. Like most of the upland Exmoor farms, the land was too poor for cereal crops and it included a hillock of grass, called the Tump , too steep even to graze sheep. People said it might have been an iron age burial mound but archaeologists had dug into the back of it one summer and found nothing.

It had been part of a small estate, Mennid Hall, and recently the land had been leased out to graze sheep, but it was now fenced off from the grounds of the Hall and word had it that the owner was short of money and nceded to sell.

" Mennid is a funny name, sounds Welsh doesn't it?

The Hall was built by an artist, Gerard Sinclair," Ellie told them. "I don't suppose you've heard of him, but he was quite famous in late Victorian times I think. It must have been a bit scandalous, he ran a nature cult up there or something, ceremonies in the woods and people running around naked, that sort of thing. Someone wrote a book about it. Anyway, it's his grandson Anthony who has it now and it's just run down, the Hall is divided up and there are workshops in the out- buildings. He's getting on a bit and I guess he's selling the farm to keep the Hall going."

When Henry and Marie caught each other's eye across the table, a spark ignited.

"Shall we just go round and have a look?"

"There's no problem with that is there? It wouldn't be trespassing or anything?"

Their farming friends laughed at their enthusiasm. They didn't take it seriously, there was no harm in a little day-dreaming while you're on holiday. They finished their lunch and parted with a warm invitation for the visitors to come over to Handy Cross before they went home.

"Well, shall we see if we can find it?" Henry asked as they got back into the car.

"Yes, it'd be interesting to see what the house is like," Marie was just a little excited.

Henry and Marie found the overgrown gateway off the lane leading out of the village and drove up to the house, originally a cottage with a large extension in the Georgian style, long sash windows and a heavy oak door with a strange knocker shaped like a goat's head.

"This house is a lot older than Victorian," Marie

surmised. " He must have bought the farm and then built the Hall on part of the land. I wonder why here, it would have been a  long way from civilisation."

"Part of the Romantic Movement I guess," Henry replied. " After all, the poets all came to Exmoor didn't they, Wordsworth, Shelley, Coleridge wrote Kubla Khan not far from here. And anyway, if you want to start a cult you want a bit of privacy I imagine!"

They spent the rest of the afternoon peering into the windows through dirty glass  and pushing open creaking old barn doors while the children ran round in the neglected fields and climbed the Tump.

A young vixen  lived under the  dilapidated chicken shed where a  slight  delicious aroma still lingered.  She watched the goings on without much concern, people had been before, an estate agent and once another couple in a new SUV but they had not stayed long. She lay on the warm earth, resting her chin on her paws, idly aware of the rabbits scuffing their hind feet in the hedgerow behind, but she wasn't hungry and was unwilling to stir before the chill air of  evening roused her.

 She was aware of her belly, heavy with the cubs which would soon be born. She would retreat into the new earth dug deep beneath the roots  of a big beech tree on one of the  field boundaries and  keep to the den, nursing her cubs, fed by their father, the dog fox she had welcomed to the territory during the winter. Two of the siblings she had helped to raise would also support her; the others of that litter  had dispersed to find territories of their own. Her father who was old now and fending for himself since her mother had died, would mostly lie up in the family's original den deep in the woods. Maintaining several earths within a shared territory was a safe strategy.

For now she was warm and content, her coat rufus and glossy in the last rays of the sun. The rabbits, plump and brindled brown, would usually have been grazing on the overgrown lawn at the front of the house, but now emerged into the orchard, only darting back, showing their white scuts, when Jack and Chloe came through the broken wooden gate.

"Look," pointed Jack, "Rabbits, lots of them."

"Oh there are baby ones," cried Chloe, watching them hop away, less wary than the full grown coneys, "I wish they'd stay, I didn't get to see them properly."

The children were attracted by the noisy flapping of a pheasant disturbed by their voices, and they got a good look at him as he strutted stiff legged down the hedge line, his green feathers bright in the late sunlight, not alarmed enough to make the clumsy effort to take flight.

"Well, what do you think?" their parents asked the children, hardly daring to raise the question in earnest themselves. It was such a big project, so impractical, and yet somehow they were encouraged, there was something in the quiet air of the place, an atmosphere of expectant calm which seemed to welcome them and draw them in.

"I love it," said Jack decisively, "I don't want to go yet."

"It's getting dark, love," Marie said, "But I'm sure we will be back." That conviction came unbidden, as if from the place itself.

At the rented cottage, the modern interior reminded

them  how much work  was needed at Holtbourne on both the house and buildings, but Henry and Marie sat down to do the  sums.

"If we could sell the house for...and we owe this much on the mortgage..."

Henry said he thought he could work  from home and go back into the office periodically, though Marie privately had her doubts about that. With so many unknowns they nevertheless went round to the estate agents the following morning to ask the price and arrange a viewing.

"Ah, Holtbourne, yes Simon is handling that one."

The receptionist asked them to take a seat and in a few minutes a middle-aged man with a friendly smile came over to shake hands.

"Mr. and Mrs. Freeman? You're interested in Holtbourne I understand?"

"We couldn't find it listed online," Henry told him.

"Ah, no, well the owner didn't want people wandering over the place and poking around."

Henry and Marie exchanged surreptitious glances; that was exactly what they had been doing after all.

"He's a bit eccentric to be honest, values his privacy and all that, although it's all fenced off now and the Hall itself is quite some distance from the farm, it's surrounded by a sort of country park. Still, you have to respect the client's wishes, but if we can't advertise online these days, it's much harder to market a property."

The asking price was considerably more than they were likely to get for their home, and   renovations would be expensive but Henry and Marie thought they could take on a bigger mortgage.

"So has there been any serious interest?" they asked.

"There aren't many original Exmoor properties left. Ever since the 1980's there's been a wave of people moving down, and anything with land is always sought after, especially to keep horses."

A viewing was arranged for later that afternoon and when the ornate key turned in the lock and they stepped into the wide hall, Henry and Marie were struck by the faded grandeur of the extended part of the house. High ceilings and cornices in the large drawing room with its white marble fireplace and polished wooden boards contrasted with the traditional farm house kitchen with its flag stone floor. Here massive old beams bore the marks of hooks for hanging herbs and game and an old Rayburn was installed in the deep brick fireplace with an oven and hotplates and a back boiler to provide hot water. That would definitely have to go. There was no gas in the village but the agent assured them that the electrics had been updated, a new consumer unit had been installed when the house had been rented out some time ago.

A scullery and pantry led off the kitchen, with a boot room opening onto the back porch and the farm yard. Upstairs were three big bedrooms, a bathroom that had seen better days, and a large attic room with a dormer window facing the fields and the mysterious Tump at the back of the house.

The sun was going down when the agent's Subaru pulled out onto the lane and a pale moon was rising. As Henry and Marie rounded up the children and Taffy, watchful crows peered down from the scotch pines at the gate.

"Listen to them," Henry told the children, and they all paused to hear the repeated soft hoarse cawing of the female sitting on her nest.

"It's her version of the pigeons cooing," Marie said, and the children laughed. The vixen sniffed the unfamiliar scents wafting towards the ruined chicken shed, even the squirrels settling for the night in the oak tree behind the barn sensed something new was afoot but the animals felt no cause for concern, these people felt right.

Josh and Thomas were amazed when Henry called, full of excitement, with the news that they were considering buying Holtbourne.

"That was quick," said Thomas. "Have you really thought about this ? Come over tomorrow and I'll talk you through a few things, this isn't something to rush into you know."

Short of telling them they were total idiots, Thomas and Ellie tried to point out the pitfalls of hill farming, even with a decent acreage and several generations of farming experience behind you. Marie and Henry listened attentively, asking sensible questions and seeming to take it in, but they were not put off.

As they were leaving, after several hours and many cups of tea, Josh came into the kitchen with Jack and Chloe who had been helping with all the chores which had been left to him.

"So, what have you decided then?" he asked, looking at the faces around the table.

"Oh we're going to make an offer," Henry confirmed, while Marie thanked Ellie for her hospitality. As they were getting into the car Josh said,

"Well, you can always look to us for any advice and a helping hand if you do go ahead, you know that," and waved them off cheerfully.

"What did you want to go saying that for?" Thomas rounded on him. "It'll be a blooming disaster anyone can see that. Don't go encouraging them!"

"Too late for that I'd say," his brother replied and then, "Dog's obedient enough anyway. You can tell a lot by the way a man trains a dog. And the kids are nice enough."

In fact it had been Marie who had done much of the dog training.

"Well just remember, we have our place to run, we can't go on too many fools' errands over there, that's all. Have you cleaned out the water trough in Beeches? I'd best do it now then."

# Chapter 3

When Henry and Marie got home the reaction to their news was hardly more encouraging. Their friends were incredulous; some were a bit envious, others could imagine nothing worse than struggling to make a living in all weathers miles from the nearest cinema, shopping mall or gym.

When they told their families the response was almost hostile. They were throwing away all that they had worked for, taking the children out of a good school, giving up the house they had so long planned and saved for. They had a modern home and job security and they were throwing all that away for what? A run down farm house, a few fields and a very uncertain future.

"It's not as if you know anything about farming," Marie's mother reasoned. "You can't just expect to keep cows or whatever, there's TB to worry about. I saw a programme about it."

"It won't be cows Mum," Marie explained patiently. "We'll have sheep and goats and keep chickens. I think farming may be in my blood, I've been thinking about what grandad told me about the farm in Jamaica."

"Don't bring that up," her mother was getting exasperated, "You know very well he and uncle Jimmy came to England because they couldn't make a living over there. Your grandad trained as a motor mechanic, and luckily he was good at it. The closest he got to farming after that was his allotment which is a very different proposition. In fact the garden in Jamaica was more like an allotment than what you are trying to do, there's no comparison."

Her father left it to his wife to argue her out of it, since she had plenty of objections to make, only saying he hoped they wouldn't jump into anything and let the dust settle before making any big decisions. He did observe that he had taken Henry for a sensible man and this was out of character. It took a conversation with Henry himself to convince Marie's parents that this wasn't just some fanciful idea of hers.

Things did not go any more smoothly with Henry's family. It didn't help that his father was an accountant; he ended up washing his hands of the whole affair, saying he wished them well but he could see them having lost everything inside five years, if they got that far, and they were not to come to him for a bale out.

"It's as if Dad is trying to live his life over again through Margaret and me. He wasn't that successful really but he thinks we should be high flyers, as if material success is all there is," Henry complained as they drove away from his parents' detached house, in a long street lined with arts and crafts style executive homes.

This reaction was sobering for Henry and Marie of course and they wavered over one weekend, but somehow the prospect of continuing as they were seemed impossible. They called the local estate agent and were pleasantly surprised at the premium brought by a substantial 1930's semi, in the catchment area for a good primary school, an advantage they would no longer be needing.

Briefly they even talked about clearing the mortgage and living on a houseboat for a while if the farm fell through, but their offer, considerably lower than the asking price, was accepted in principle and that clinched it.

On the phone, the agent, Simon, told them that Mr. Sinclair had turned down a good offer from a wealthy business man whom he suspected of wanting to demolish the house and redevelop the entire site. He was apparently prepared to accept a reduced price on the assurance that the land would continue to be farmed traditionally.

Good property in the city was in short supply and it didn't take long for serious buyers to make an offer. Marie felt a tinge of regret, looking around the lovely home she and Henry had created ; after all, Chloe had been born in that house, but she quelled the nostalgia, this was going to be a whole new life.

They used a broker to negotiate an agricultural mortgage, which, while advantageous, was still going to be a stretch and sat down once more to go through the figures.

" It's going to be tight. We're going to have to make it pay, you know," Henry said. "My salary alone won't hack it once we've spent the contingency money."

"I know," Marie agreed, "but we've given ourselves a year and we'll only pay for essential work for now. We can do a lot ourselves."

When they had exchanged, Marie gave in her notice at work, which was a big step. There was no going back now.

She had been too preoccupied with her own affairs to think much about Sally, although they had exchanged a few texts. With the move now imminent she was anxious to see her and catch up in person. Perhaps they could meet in town for a coffee? Marie was surprised when Sally replied that she was at home that afternoon, it was a weekday after all, but she put off writing up the notes from a school visit and drove across town. Sally lived in an expensive area and Marie suspected that she was paying more than her fair share of the rent on their flat in a tall Georgian house. Matthew sold IT software solutions but Marie had gathered that he didn't earn very much.

Her first impression when Sally opened the door was that her friend had lost more weight. She was wearing a long sweater although it was early June and although her chestnut hair was still thick and lustrous, she was pale and her cheekbones seemed more pronounced. Marie hugged her affectionately.

"Are you alright? You don't look well."

"I'm fine," Sally replied, turning away to lead her through into the living room, but the light from the tall windows clearly revealed the shadows under her blue eyes.

"It's good to see you," she said, "Have a seat, I'll make some tea."

Marie looked around the room which was immaculate, nothing out of place, no signs of a life being lived in fact. It was like a show home. Sally was back with the tea, curling herself up on the sofa and cradling her mug in both hands.

"So you're really going to do it? I was thinking we should do another spread and see what the cards have to say."

Marie was grateful for the offer so she let Sally lay out the deck without probing any more, although she had some trouble clearing her mind to concentrate on the cards lying face down on the coffee table.
This time she had something definite to ask.

"Are we doing the right thing taking on the farm?" She drew four significant cards. The first was The Wheel of Fortune, a clear sign to trust and take the plunge, with the proviso of the next card, the Nine of Wands indicating the need for courage; they would have to push through barriers and persevere. The Four of Wands was very encouraging, indicating a new home, stability and firm foundations , happiness and security, a vision beginning to be realised. The Fourth card was the Moon, mysterious, feminine and passive in nature. Sally told her that  this hinted at something hidden to be revealed in the future. Marie did not know what to make of that last card but she made notes from the reading so she could refer back to it later.

Marie thanked Sally for interpreting the cards but this time she was not prepared to be deflected from her concern.

"So you're not at work today then?" She wondered if Sally was ill.

"Oh, I'm not with Listons any more, I've left."

This was a surprise, Sally was a research chemist, highly paid, with the added advantage of speaking fluent German, since her family had lived in Zurich.

"What? Why did you leave?"

"It was getting too much travelling to work every day. The trains kept getting cancelled and if I went on the bus it was always late. I wasn't getting there on time and then I'd be late home."

Late home for what, Marie wondered, there were no children to collect from nursery.

"I'm working from home now doing technical translations for an agency."

"That can't be very interesting surely," Marie protested, "and not as well paid. You always managed the journey before, what's changed?"

Sally shifted awkwardly in her seat and then stood up to go to the window, turning her back while she said.

"I had to leave before Matthew in the mornings and and then if I was late home it was difficult. He likes to eat early."

So that was it, it was obvious now, Matthew was tightening his grip.

"Sally, you can't go on like this. You need to get out, you're twenty eight, you've got a life to live."

"Oh we do go out," Sally chose to misinterpret her meaning. "We go into town and do the shopping on Saturdays, and Matthew likes to go to car rallies, so we're often out on a Sunday."

Marie remembered that Sally didn't even drive, so motor sport could hardly interest her.

She was about to get Sally to open up further, but they heard a key turn in the lock and heavy footsteps in the hall. Marie noticed that not only was Sally suddenly standing to attention but that she herself was on her feet facing the door.

'He's got me at it now' she thought, 'We're like

rabbits in the headlights.' She realised it was past five'clock and Matthew was home.

He was taken aback for a moment when he saw Marie.

"Oh,you're here, are you ?" passive aggressive, a plain acknowledgement of fact. He walked across the room, coming between her and Sally so that she had to step aside, and putting his arm round Sally's waist, kissed her and drew her so close into his side that her body was bent into his hip.

Marie glanced at Sally's now glacial expression,unsure what to do next.

"What's for dinner Babe? I'm starving." Matthew said.

"It's ready to go in the oven, I'll turn it on."

He released Sally and she went into the kitchen.

"You're moving away then? Where is it you're going?"

"We're moving to Exmoor."

" We won't be seeing so much of you in future then."

His gaze was unsettling but she felt like standing her ground. Marie was in no hurry to go home, the children were with her mother. She almost sat down again but there was a tension in the air and she knew it would only make things more awkward for Sally if she stayed.

"You must have a lot to do, don't let us keep you. Sally's such a chatterbox. Come and say goodbye to your friend," he called.

Sally reappeared, hovering in the doorway and Marie had no alternative but to leave. She drew Sally with her into the hall, calling goodbye cheerfully as a cover for whispering,

"For heaven's sake Sally, this is making you ill. You've got to get rid of him, he's sucking you dry." Describing her afternoon to Henry later, Marie was angry, almost as much with Sally as with Matthew.

"When I first met her at the craft institute she was bubbly, radiant, full of fun. Now she's like a ghost."

"I remember her, she came to some of our barbecues didn't she? She has got family, though?"

Marie nodded.

"Her parents divorced and her dad still lives in Zurich. Her mother is in England, though not round here. I don't think she sees much of her. It's such a shame,she had a real talent for pottery; with her chemistry background  she was inventing new glazes, then she gave all that up."

"She didn't have to," Henry reminded her, "You stuck with your weaving and got the spinning wheel. I know you don't have much time for it at the moment but all that is important to you. Maybe she just wasn't that keen."

"You haven't met him, he's like a snake," Marie told him.

"Well, she can always come and see us when we're settled, maybe a break away from him would help." Henry stood up, stretching, having said all he could on the subject.

"She can't even get out to the shops on her own, let alone as far as Exmoor."

Marie was suddenly conscious of her own good fortune. She came over, placing her palms against his chest, reaching up to kiss his face.

"I'm so lucky to have you," she told him. He laughed, holding her close and squeezing her bottom.

"Just keep that in mind," he told her, "When I've dragged you off to where the wild things are."

"We're dragging each other," she assured him, "And I just can't wait!"

Marie and Henry left the children with her parents for a long weekend and went down to do some thorough cleaning before the move. They pitched a tent in the garden and on the first evening cleaned the bathroom as thoroughly as they could so they would at least have somewhere to wash.

"It's not as if it's filthy," Marie said, "It's just that everything is so old. The surface has gone on this bath, we'll have to replace that."

Henry examined the chipped enamel she had been scrubbing and said,

" It might be worth having it re-enamelled. It's a really big bath and solid cast iron. You'd pay a lot for one as good. I can't imagine how they got it up those stairs; you'd have to take a sledge hammer to it to remove it. Hell of a job."

"The wash basin has a few hairline cracks," Marie pointed out, "But I reckon it's original 1930's and that's back in fashion. It's actually not too bad, and the toilet's OK if we get a new seat."

"There you are then," Henry was pleased, "Replace the cracked tiles, get rid of the old lino, a lick of paint, Job's a good'un as they say in these parts."

Sitting in the tent with the door open after a supper cooked on the camping stove, they were looking out

41

across the fields when Marie became aware of movement on the far slope.

"There are animals up there," she touched his arm, dropping her voice to a whisper, "Quite a few of them. That farmer isn't still grazing his cattle here is he?"

"No, that was only sheep and anyway there was nothing here this afternoon, we'd have noticed. These are bigger, where's the flash light?"

When they shone a beam across the field, a cluster of bright eyes were reflected back, all turned curiously in their direction.

"They're red deer," Henry exclaimed, and then, laughing, "And they're eating our grass!"

"Well, they're welcome to it, we don't have any use for it yet, they'll keep it down for us." Marie was delighted to think nature was so close to their doorstep.

Redirecting the light as the deer retreated up into the wood, Henry made out three young stags with pricket horns, not old enough to grow a full rack of antlers.

"The hinds split up in May and June to have their calves so we probably won't see many of them now. I remember Granddad telling me the stags form bachelor groups except in October during the rut, but anyway the deer don't usually form big herds. I don't think they'll be a problem to us even when we have our own stock. The deer move around the moor and it's not as if we are going to have corn to trample. Just as well, deer fencing costs a fortune."

"We may have to fence the garden properly though," Marie replied, "And you don't want them in your poly tunnels next year."

"Oh, they won't come that close to the house, they're

wary of humans."

Henry was sure they could live and let live, after all the deer were here first, he thought.

Later that night they were disturbed by loud snuffling and grunting. Waking suddenly, Marie was frightened for a moment, thinking they had wild boar in the garden, though they had never heard of any on Exmoor. Turning on the flash light again, they saw nothing more alarming than a family of badgers, two adults and three cubs, foraging quite unconcerned in the pool of light from the torch.

"We must be in their territory, I expect they have a sett in the wood," Henry said. "I reckon we'll see them about the place all the time."

"We're not getting much sleep are we?" Marie grumbled, "If we get the house cleaned tomorrow maybe we should sleep indoors."

Next morning they managed to light the ancient Rayburn with some wood they found in one of the sheds and the back boiler produced enough hot water to do some serious cleaning.

After a couple of days of hard work the place was habitable, floorboards and cupboards scrubbed, walls washed down and they sat down on the stairs with mugs of tea to take stock. Marie was sorry for the house as if it were a living entity.

"We can sand the floors and make painting the walls a priority," Henry said. "It's just really shabby and neglected, isn't it?"

"Whoever the last tenants were, they must have led a pretty spartan life here, but it was probably OK with a fire going in the Rayburn and food in the oven."

"We can do better than that," Henry assured her,
" We'll make it comfortable you'll see." But it was still a
very basic home they moved into.

# Chapter 4

Before mid-summer two U Drive vans were turning off the M5 at Taunton and heading across country towards Exmoor and a new life.

Late on the first evening,after the children had fallen happily into bed, Henry and Marie sat outside on two faded wicker chairs they had found in a barn. They were sharing a bottle of Prosecco, exhausted but too keyed up to sleep without some down time first.

"I really think we did manifest this you know,"Marie told him, continuing a thread of conversation which had run throughout those extraordinary months.

"You mean, you think we have called all this into being?" he teased, not quite convinced by her familiar train of thought.

"Not by an effort of will, but by being, or becoming, who we are meant to be," she was serious. "It was all here before of course for centuries, with its own agenda , all the birds and animals, plants, trees all with their own existence. We are so lucky that it hasn't been changed, ruined for profit, that it's still here for us to enjoy. We're its new custodians. I think we were chosen in a way, but we had to be up for it, to show we were worthy."

Henry laughed, looking at her affectionately in her yellow cotton sundress, brown wavy hair with its golden glints twisted up in a scrunchy, his Marie. There was no-one like her, brave and independent, resourceful and optimistic.

"Well, it isn't exactly a crock of gold we've been

handed," he said, "And I guess it's untouched because it's been on the edge of things, like all the Exmoor farms; not worth grubbing out the hedgerows to make big fields like in Norfolk, thank God, that's what makes it timeless."

They lapsed into silence, drinking the last of their wine and gazing up at the vast array of stars wheeling overhead and letting the peace of the place soak into their tired bodies. The light from the kitchen window hardly reached beyond their chairs, and their eyes had become accustomed to the darkness. Something rustled in the hedge, the old dog fox slipped soundlessly across the orchard, and two of the badgers snuffled noisily across the grass, unperturbed by the humans sitting still and rapt as they became aware of all the night life around them. An tawny owl hooted in the oak tree, so close that it made them jump and then laugh at themselves.

"Come on, time for bed I think," said Henry, pulling Marie up from her seat. They turned back into the house, arms around each other's waist, tired but happy.

After a few days spent unpacking, Marie set off to the local shops for some provisions. She took Jack and Chloe with her, who were keen to see the recreation ground with its play area and tennis courts. In the bakers she was greeted with some curiosity; word had got round that there were new owners at Holtbourne, and the village gossip machine had cranked into gear.

"These are your children then? How old are they?"

"Jack is 10 and Chloe is 8," Marie replied.

Glancing at her offspring she suddenly rather wished

she had smartened them up a bit before presenting them for judgement to the village, but raising her chin she defied the idea, 'take us as you find us' she thought. The assistant was smiling though.

"That's good news," she said. "We'll get one more year out of this young man before senior school I expect? You are sending them to the village school?"

"Hope so, isn't there room?" She had looked at the website and emailed the school after all.

This was one aspect it had not occurred to Marie to check.

"Oh yes! That's the point, if numbers fall below fifty they start talking about closing it and we have to start a campaign all over again."

"Well, we can swell the numbers then," Marie replied, relieved to find there was one definite positive to their arrival in the eyes of the village.

It was not as if they had swanned in and bought a holiday home, but she was just beginning to be aware of an underlying attitude about locals and incomers; she had sensed a hint of it from the plumber who had come round to discuss replacing the ancient Rayburn with a reconditioned oil fired Aga.

As they headed for the more neutral territory of the small supermarket she wondered how many decades it took to really fit in. She need not have worried unduly because Mrs. Headley, the arbiter of village opinion, reported to her next customer that she was a bit 'hippyish' but there was 'no side to her.'

They had intended to give the children the last few weeks of term off school to settle in, but with the small traditional stone building plainly in sight, Marie took the children into reception to register. The receptionist was all smiles, spoke kindly to the children and sat them down where they could look into the playground and see the pupils running around shouting since it was break time while Marie filled out some forms.

As it turned out the headmistress, who also taught the top two years combined, was drinking her coffee in her little office, visible through a glass partition, so there was no need for an appointment for an interview; she simply introduced herself to the children and suggested they come in on Monday and get settled in before the holidays.

Used to the formality of a large city academy, Jack and Chloe took this casual suggestion in their stride and, well pleased with such an uncomplicated arrangement, Marie took the children round to the rec where they tried out all the equipment and she got into conversation with two young mothers with toddlers who filled her in on some more details of village life.

Marie suddenly realised the whole morning had gone and hurried the children home to see how Daddy was getting on without them. She need not have worried that he was battling on alone because she opened the kitchen door to find him sitting comfortably at the kitchen table talking to an old man in a woolly hat with several days of non-designer stubble on his chin. This individual immediately struggled to his feet and made as if to leave, but Marie's warm smile and a suggestion that she put the kettle on reassured him and soon she was hearing the momentous news of their
discovery in the machine shed.

George Binnicombe had farmed at Owey on the other side of the village, but was now living alone in one of the retirement bungalows down the lane. He had wandered over on his daily walk to see what these new folks were like and  the sight of the old Volvo had emboldened him to peer into the workshop where Henry was repairing the orchard gate. George stood watching him for a few moments before he knocked on the open door, remarking,

"You're making a fair job of that," by way of introduction.

A tour of the yard had followed, with George telling Henry how things had been when there had been a farm manager with a family living in the house.

"It was quite productive in those days," he said. "There was a dairy herd so they laid on electricity and water to the buildings, that was when we had the milk marketing board and you could make a profit out of a few Friesians. There was a groundsman and gardeners round at the Hall, it was all kept up, not like nowadays when it's just going wild more or less. There are young people living in the house with workshops round the back, though I don't think they make much of a living out of their craft stuff. The forge does well enough making railings and gates and a bit of fancy metal work, weathervanes and such.  Mr. Sinclair just lives in part of the Hall now and the rest is a sort of commune you might say. They're pleasant enough if you meet them though."

When they got round to the machine shed and dragged the heavy door back, Henry had pointed to a stack of rotting hay across the end,

"That's another job I'll have to get round to, hauling that lot out and burning it."

"Yes, it would never have been good hay to start with. When the land was rented out after Harold left it would just be sheep hay for the ewes overwintering here," George told him.

And that was when George pulled one of the bales out of the corner and said,

"Well, I'll be damned, it looks as if the machinery is still here. Look, there's the Fergie, well, I'll be blowed."

The attachments were lying there next to the tractor and George's opinion was that there was not much wrong with any of it, since it had been protected from the weather.

"Most of these restoration projects you see, the stuff has been outside for years, but we could get the Fergie going I reckon and it'd be fine for what you want."

Henry took the mention of 'we' on board with gratitude and they retreated to the kitchen to talk it over.

When Marie returned they were discussing the tricky question of ownership.

"You bought the place lock, stock and barrel didn't you?" George said. "It stands to reason anything in the barns is yours."

"Well it certainly wasn't on the inventory," Henry said, "But then neither was all the other stuff that was left lying around. I don't see anyone laying claim to it, do you?"

George stayed for a scratch lunch of pork pie, salad and chips and by the time he left, he and Henry were committed to stripping down the Fergie's engine and getting her going.

'As if I haven't got enough on.' but Henry pushed the endless list of jobs waiting to the back of his mind, this was going to be an asset.

Luckily in those first few weeks the weather was perfect, though the farmers were worrying about rain for their crops. Henry's boss had reluctantly agreed to him taking a month's holiday; he had rather played down his move to the country and working from home was technically feasible.

They got the broadband up and running; fortunately it was reliable due to a local initiative to support rural communities and while the children were at school he was able to work in the sitting room. By the time school broke up he had been able to make an office area in the back of the large stone barn at the side of the property. There was a window to the rear and while it would definitely need some insulation and a means of heating in the winter, he installed his desk and tacked up some painted plasterboard and even hung a picture to give the impression of a proper office for team and Zoom meetings.

The children settled quickly at school; Jack and Chloe were confident, friendly kids and while their new life was unfamiliar they loved it all and their enthusiasm made them popular. Jack had played football at his last school and was quickly introduced to the village junior team. Henry's father had given him an expensive mountain bike for his birthday before the move, saying,

"The boy may as well have something useful, there won't be any cycle paths where you're going," so he was able to go off into the woods with his new friends during the long evenings, though the bike soon lost some of its shiny paintwork.

Chloe found a circle of girls to play with at school although there were not many close to her in age and a couple of those were best friends so there was some adjustment to fit a new girl into the group. Marie intended to make sure that various children were invited individually over the holidays to foster closer friendships for her two.

Jack had asked for the attic bedroom  at the back of the house, facing the Tump. Attics of course are notoriously cold in winter and hot in summer so now he always kept the window open at night. Soon after they moved in, shortly before mid-summer, he was lying in bed facing the square of light as the sun finally went down and twilight brought the first glimmer of stars in the patch of sky framed by the dormer.

He became aware of a sound like music,almost too faint to hear and went to look out. He could see deer who had come down off the hill, a group of hinds with their calves, standing motionless, all gazing towards the Tump. Jack listened intently but could not quite distinguish the notes, either because it was too far away or almost too high pitched for his ears. Other animals seemed attracted he realised, badgers, rabbits, even the foxes whom he glimpsed regularly about the farm were gathering in various places as if fascinated by the Tump itself. As Jack concentrated, he thought it was a tinkling, piping sound not shrill but thrilling to hear.

He did not know how long he stood at the window but at last the sound stopped, the spell was broken and the animals began to disperse and go about their nightly business as if nothing had happened. Jack was just turning away, suddenly aware of a chill breeze, when his attention was caught by something else on the hill. The moon had risen and was giving enough fitful light between high cloud for him to see a shape forming on the top of the Tump. Almost too solid for mist, it was a greyish column with a slightly golden tint and looked exactly like a tall man although there was something odd about the figure. The hips were broad, tapering to pointed feet, and his arms were raised and bent as if holding something against his chest. As Jack watched, the figure dissolved slowly and the column of mist, if that is what it was, rose into the air and disappeared. Jack was fascinated rather than disturbed and was determined to watch and see if it happened again. He sat up expectantly on subsequent nights and witnessed the scene again on mid-summer's eve and the following night, always presaged by the sound of the music. Again the animals gathered and again the figure formed and dispersed, though the animals seemed to lose attention once the music had stopped, as if they could not distinguish the visible source of the melody.

As mid-summer passed it happened only occasionally, but Jack was always alerted by the faint sound of the notes and in time he began to have a feeling at the end of some days that conditions were right, though he could not say exactly how he knew. Indeed he said nothing to anyone about his experiences, partly because he didn't want to have to listen to anyone trying to explain it away and also because it just seemed too precious, too personal to share.

He did point out the wisps of mist to his father which

appeared on the wooded hillside at the head of their combe on cool mornings, always rising like smoke from the same spots, before the heat of the day. Henry thought there must be clearings among the trees and moisture from the warm earth, damp with dew, must be evaporating there and rising into view. That seemed reasonable to Jack but it did not make him doubt his own much more intense experiences.

# Chapter 5

Meanwhile those first weeks saw a lot of progress with decorating  inside and repairs to the buildings; the Aga was installed and George was as good as his word and supervised the restoration of the tractor which had a simple engine by modern standards. Henry followed instructions and found parts on line and one weekend Marie's uncle Gary, who was a motor mechanic like his father, came down and between the three of them they got the Fergie going.

It took some detective work to understand the water system. The stream serving the farm was spring fed, emerging somewhere on the moor above and filtered through the peat. It meandered between the trees at the head of the combe, becoming a brook which served most of the fields before part of it had been channelled into a well-like structure in the yard from which it was piped in various directions to the larger outbuildings and into a rather unsavoury tank in the back scullery where it was gravity fed around the house.

Replacing this tank with a stainless steel container was a priority, but at least the water was tested every year and had recently been confirmed pure enough to drink. Years ago,one of the local farms had apparently been found to have such a high copper content in the water that the GP had noticed the blonde daughters' hair was developing a green tint, like mermaids. Luckily no high mineral content was found at Holtbourne, in fact in the past the manager had sold bottled water for a while when it had first become popular; the spring was even believed to have healing properties.

This made sense of the name of the holding which appeared in the Domesday Book, Holt meaning wood and Bourne meaning water. Like most upland farms, the house had been built in the sheltered base of the combe, facing away from the prevailing West wind and the near fields were fairly flat, the further pasture rising gently to the woodland which bounded the property as the combe narrowed and became steeper. Unlike some of the closed combes, theirs had a bridle path running up from the lane which made access to the moorland above easier but it was some way over the heather and gorse across tracks and sheep paths before it joined a road across the top.

As time went on, friends and family visited. Some were helpful and got stuck in clearing barns and ditches and helping to mend fences. Others just brought deli food, bottles of wine and news of city life so that Henry and Marie were forced to down tools and relax for a few days and take a much needed break.

On one cooler evening in July when friends were staying, Henry decided to light a fire and try out the chimney. The room immediately filled with smoke and someone started poking about up the chimney with the fire irons. A heap of twigs and sticks descended down the chimney with a rush and there was a squirrel's drey in the hearth. Luckily the nest had extinguished the fire but the hearth was full of soot and dust and there were 3 little kits in the drey.

"Oh No," cried Chloe, rushing over, "Poor little

things, we've got to save them!"

Everyone crowded round to look, they were virtually hairless, tiny and helpless.

"Ok, I've got it," said Henry, "Get me a dustbin lid. Nobody touch them, the mother will abandon them if she smells humans."

He carefully scooped up the drey, placing it on the upturned dustbin lid and carrying it carefully outside he placed it on top of the oil tank newly installed at the side of the house. They shut their cats and Taffy inside and the children kept watch for half an hour, ready to shoo any predator away, until the mother appeared and removed the kits one by one in her mouth, to the safety of a crook in the beech tree, watched by the humans through the sitting room window.

"I know a lot of country people hate squirrels and think they're vermin, and some of the farmers will shoot or poison foxes, but our wildlife is precious," said Marie and their friends took the story back home, feeling they had had an experience of country life you don't get staying in a B&B.

George had introduced Henry to the regulars in the public bar down at the Plough Inn and as the tractor restoration attracted some interest, it was not long before he felt comfortable going in on his own and passing the time of day with the crowd, most of them from third generation village families.

It did not take long for someone to suggest he could come over and net the rabbit holes in the banks, putting ferrets down to flush out some tasty coneys. Haunch of rabbit tasted like chicken, he said, and offered to share the catch with the family. Someone else asked if he could bring his son over for some rough shooting later in the year, but Henry rejected both offers as politely as he could. The thought of persecuting the innocent wild creatures living trustfully on their land seemed like a complete betrayal to him, but he was aware that made him look soft to the local men. There seemed to be a balance of nature he said. He did not mention the foxes they were harbouring because they were considered vermin by everyone.

"Daft beggar, thinks he can come down here and take up farming," the ferrets' owner grumbled after Henry had left the bar. He could get good money for fat rabbits from the gastro pub at the other end of the village where saddle of rabbit in a wild mushroom sauce featured at high prices on the menu. You can find chanterelles in the Exmoor woods if you know where to look.

"Your William wouldn't want the place though, would he?" someone asked.

"Nah, not enough land with it, he's better off contracting, and anyway Kayleigh wouldn't move their kids into that old house. They're after one of those new ones they're building for local couples, you buy part of it and pay some rent on the rest."

"Shared Equity," someone said.

"Yes, that's it."

Not that Henry had much time for the pub, it was becoming increasingly difficult to balance working from home with getting things done on the farm. He took the mobile out with him if he needed to do something on the land during the day but the signal was not always reliable and he had missed calls, and often he was over in the makeshift office catching up on the laptop late into the evening. He was finding remote meetings more tiring than he had expected.

Every few weeks he had to drive back to the city and spend three days in the office, staying over with his parents, whose one visit so far had not been a success; they were at no pains to disguise their disapproval. His father had reservations about the septic tank and was convinced the first autumn gale would bring half the slates off the roof.

"There can't be a proper damp course," he complained, "and God knows what's holding this end wall together."

"Well Dad," Henry rejoined wearily, fed up with the constant criticism, " it's stood for at least the last three hundred years so I guess it'll see us out."

His mother did a tour of inspection with Marie and having condemned the kitchen and scullery as 'medieval' conceded that the sitting room at least could be elegant with some replastering and several litres of Farrell and Ball paint.

That weekend, when George wandered up from his bungalow, he hesitated by the gate, seeing a new BMW parked outside and a tall distinguished looking man talking to Jack who was hanging his head as if he was getting a lecture. He turned back unnoticed and walked another way; these were not the kind of visitors he wanted to meet.

When Josh and Thomas came over to see the tractor they were surprised at how much Henry and Marie had achieved.

"You have tidied the place up," Thomas admitted, "so

what's next?"

"Well we have to rebuild the hen house, but on a bigger scale, and we need to think about getting some sheep I suppose," Marie was not sure what breed to consider, though George had advised Exmoor Horn or Dorset ewes.

"The dispersal sales are coming up, they're always held in July. I'm going to market on Wednesday if you want to join me."

Thomas was relieved not to have been called on for advice before now and was willing to help them avoid any pitfalls in buying stock.

"I think you should start with thirty ewes, Exmoors are hardy and good mothers. We lamb as early as we can, just after Christmas to get the best prices, but I think you should wait 'til March when the weather is better. Young lambs can stand the cold if they have plenty of warm milk inside them, but they can't stand the wet, and you can't just leave them in the lambing shed if the weather turns because they start to get infections."

"We really need to learn all this, at least I do," said Marie. " Henry is still working and he wants to get a couple of poly tunnels going in the spring so it looks as if I shall be in charge of the sheep and chickens."

Josh started explaining about borrowing a ram, an older one would do for that number of ewes, and putting him in with the flock in November. The brothers suggested she came over when they were lambing and lent a hand.

"When you get the hang of it, we'll pay you if you want to do some night shifts, we're always short handed at the peak time, we have over 200 ewes to lamb in a few weeks. There'll always be someone experienced with you in the shed of course."

Marie thought that was a very generous offer and the idea of actually earning some money out of farming was particularly attractive. They were both aware how much of their savings was draining away with no return in sight.

Henry rearranged his schedule, not for the first time, and they both took a day away from the farm while the children were in school. The cattle market was busy, with pens of sheep waiting to go into the ring while the farming community gathered in the rather cheerless cafeteria eating bacon rolls and drinking weak coffee. Voices echoed round the tin roof, everyone taking advantage of a chance to socialise; farming could be a lonely business.

The Freemans were grateful to have Thomas to guide them, he chose the sheep and of course they let him do the bidding; the incessant   drone of the auctioneer's voice and nearly invisible gestures from interested parties would have been incomprehensible to them and they would never have succeeded in making a purchase by themselves, let alone of the right animals at a good price.

By early afternoon however they were the new owners of thirty three healthy young Exmoor Horn ewes, recently shorn, and an arrangement had been made with someone to bring them over later in a trailer. Henry and Marie leaned over the holding pen, admiring their curling horns and neat  little cloven hooves, almost deafened by the bleating of an entire yard full of anxious sheep.

"This is really something isn't it?" Marie said. "Who'd have thought a year ago we'd have been standing here looking at our own flock of sheep?"

"It's still hard to believe isn't it?" Henry replied. "It was a bit of a shock when Thomas suddenly suggested coming today, bit short notice, but it's time we started to stock the place and do some real farming."

By the time the trailer arrived, the children were home from school, so, leaving Taffy in the kitchen, the whole family went up to open the side gate onto the lane which gave direct access into the first of the upper fields. The ewes came down the ramp onto their new pasture, running towards the far end before gradually settling and starting to graze. Their bleating carried on the breeze down towards the house and Marie said,

"That's a sound we'll be living with every day from now on."

Those upper fields, gently sloping and free draining, had been 'topped' by Henry using the tractor, to cut down tall weeds and let the mix of edible grasses grow through. All the pasture was old ley which had not been ploughed in living memory, but in Harold's day it had been regularly harrowed and mown in rotation so that a rich mix of herbs and fescues grew together with the tougher rye grasses which traditionally made up good pasture.

At Thomas and Josh's suggestion they were going to graze the upper fields and reserve the lower fields of richer grass to grow on, now that at last there had been sufficient rain, so that they could take a hay crop in late July or early August to feed the sheep during the winter.

Ideally they would have made hay in June but that would have to be the plan for next year, and many farmers had to be satisfied with one cut after the dry spring and early summer.

In those late summer months the sheep did not require more than checking daily for lameness or fly strike, or inflamed joints caused by ticks, challenges which fortunately they were not faced with immediately. With so few sheep to look after, Marie came to know them individually and since she brought them apples, they soon came running when she appeared and she was able to move quietly among them, checking them over. Taffy would never be a working sheepdog, but she was obedient and once Marie had introduced her on the lead and she had got over her initial excitement at seeing a flowing mass of white bodies, she could be trusted to come over the farm with the family, or be left to her own devices.

George came up regularly and took pleasure in advising, giving them the benefit of his lifetime's experience. In return the odd bottle of whisky and his favourite lemon drizzle cake found their way onto his kitchen table, and sometimes Marie insisted he take a few items home when she returned from the big supermarket in town, telling him it was 'buy one, get one free.'

As time went on, Henry and Marie realised that George was scarcely managing on his old age pension but they didn't like to risk offending him by mentioning money, once he had adamantly refused to be paid for anything he did. At one point it was obvious that George had a painful tooth abscess but was refusing to go to the dentist; evidently he was  not registered and had not been for years. He was painting on oil of cloves and taking painkillers but the suffering continued. In the end Henry persuaded him to make a dental appointment and drove him into town to make sure he went. They came away with a prescription for some antibiotics and the recommendation that he have a root canal filling. On the way home George was complaining about the cost of treatment.

"These antibiotics will do the trick now, I don't need to go back. I'll cancel the next appointment, you don't need to bother about driving me in again."

Henry took the bull by the horns and mentioned pension credit. It turned out that George had picked up a leaflet from the GP surgery some time ago but it suddenly dawned on Henry that his friend could scarcely read well enough to understand the rules for claiming. He had noticed that George took a very long time filling in the registration form at the dentists, and that was comparatively simple. Here at last was something valuable they could do for George in return for all his unstinting help, provided he could broach the matter delicately.

"You need a computer to do all those things these days. Years ago you just went down to the council office," said George.

"You're right," Henry agreed, "But there is a village agent to help people  get what they're due. It isn't charity you know, it's just part of their pension for people without a lot of savings."

Of course George might be sitting on a small fortune

for all Henry knew, but just be over careful about spending it.

"Village agent? That Sarah Carter? I don't want my business spread all round the village. That husband of hers would have it all round The Plough in no time. I would never be able to show my face in there again."

Henry thought there must be a confidentiality clause in the agent's contract but it might not be water tight he had to admit. Finally he ventured,

"Well you know I have a computer, and if I could help you sort it out it would be a great pleasure to me, after all you do for us. Maybe just have a think about it eh?"

Some days later George broached the subject again while they were dismantling the dilapidated hen house, which the young vixen only occasionally visited now that she had three well grown cubs to hunt for. One evening after supper in the kitchen, George agreed to sit down with Henry and tackle the online form and a few weeks later, he burst into the kitchen beaming with delight, brandishing a confirmation letter from the DWP, somehow convinced he had beaten the system.

The plan was to rebuild the chicken house on a larger scale, adjoining the orchard where the hens could peck about freely during the day. Taffy was usually around the farmyard during the day, while the family were in and out of the buildings, and although she did not go out of her way to chase the foxes, it was a stand off and they were rightly wary of coming too close.

The chicken were to be Marie's project and she decided to go for Welsummers, being hardy and easy to keep, and good layers of colourful eggs which look 'free range'. She was hoping to sell from the gate and to the local delicatessen. Later on she also wanted to breed Bantams and Silkies because the young birds fetched good prices as pets, but they would need a proper enclosure for protection.

While the adults were always so busy, Jack and Chloe were left much to their own devices at the start of the school holidays. There were long golden days to run through the ripening grasses which rippled in the wind like waves in the sea. Overhead the twittering swallows, whose second brood had fledged from their nests in the beams of the old buildings and under the eaves, swooped low to catch insects all day, gathering on the power wires overhead as the sunset reddened and the children came in at last grubby and tired, to tell the news of their adventures.

They had heard the young buzzards screeching to their parents as they wheeled in the blue sky overhead, and in the dusk the barn owlets in their nest at the end of the big stone barn churred constantly, sounding, as Marie said, like a washing machine on the spin cycle. Henry was glad they didn't make that much noise during the day or business conferencing from his makeshift office would be almost impossible.

The overgrown garden was also the children's domain and they cleared space enough to get into the ruined fruit cage where there were plenty of raspberries and a good crop of black currants. They came out with sticky fingers and a good harvest of berries. The family had no trouble eating the raspberries themselves, but Marie was pleased to be able to sell some of the black currants to the village deli. It was hardly a great contribution to their budget but it encouraged her to think the farm was capable of yielding some income.

One day Chloe came running into the kitchen, breathless with excitement, followed by Jack carrying something which was obviously heavy in a bucket. "You'll never guess what we found!" Chloe cried. Jack dumped the bucket down on the table and hauled out a very large and ancient looking tortoise.

"We found him in the long grass," Jack explained. "He must have been around all this time and we only just spotted him."

"That's amazing," Henry agreed, heading the tortoise off as it trundled towards the end of the table.

"I suppose there's plenty for him to eat, if it is a him and not her, and it would just hibernate in a corner of one of the open sheds for the winter. It must be pretty old judging by the size of it. It must have belonged to the farm manager's children years ago."

"Well now he belongs to us!" Jack declared, "And we're going to take better care of him. Can he have some lettuce? And what about a tomato?"

Marie brought a selection of offerings out of the fridge and they set them on the flag stone floor in front of the tortoise to see what it would choose. At first it took a leisurely tour of the kitchen, but returning to the food it started to munch thoughtfully on the lettuce, its toothless mouth and pink tongue delighting the fascinated children. It took some persuading to get Chloe and Jack to put the animal back where they had found it.

"Don't worry, he must like the garden or he'd have left years ago. This is his home and now you know he's here you won't have any difficulty finding him again," Marie insisted, sending them back out with their prize.

One advantage to the discovery was that Jack took to mowing the lawn regularly and tidied the overgrown borders in order to keep track of Hercules as they called their new pet, since Google identified him as a Greek spur-thighed tortoise.

Shortly afterwards there was an incident which worried Marie. The garden borders started to be cleared, and hardy plants  like Japanese Anemones, Montbretia and large white Marguerites were coming into flower, having survived years of neglect.

On the way home from town, Marie called in at the garden centre on impulse and decided to buy a yellow climbing rose to plant against the back wall and a wisteria to train over the front door to relieve the plain exterior of the house.

Queuing to pay, she noticed a set of wind chimes on a rack beside the till, reduced from £34.99 to £18. It was another item they could ill afford, but it was a bargain and she suddenly liked the thought of the gentle tinkling sound whenever the wind blew. It would make the place more homely she decided and added them to her trolley. When Marie got home she showed her plants to Henry and asked him to hang the wind chimes from the corner of the back porch. He was up a stepladder screwing in a bracket when the children came by and without warning Jack erupted, shouting,

"What are you doing? Take them down, they're horrible! They'll drown it all out with that racket!"

He was beside himself with desperation,

"Don't let it make that noise, it's not the real thing, it's disgusting!"

His parents stared at him, amazed at this sudden display of passion, and Chloe was so shocked she burst into tears. Amid the uproar Henry unhooked the offending ornament and brought it down again.

"Alright son,look, it's just wind chimes, see, they jingle together when the wind blows. Your Mum likes them, what's the harm? If we get tired of them, we can take them down again."

"No,no, it's all wrong, it's a terrible noise, it'll frighten it all away."

Jack ran indoors and they could hear his steps running up the two flights of stairs and his bedroom door banging hard enough to take it off its hinges. Henry and Marie looked at one another dumbfounded.

Chloe struggled out of the comfort of her mother's arms and turned indoors to find her brother, while their parents tried to make sense of the scene they had just witnessed.

"What's got into him? It's like he was possessed!" said Henry.

Marie was seriously concerned.

"You know, maybe it's a kind of sensory overload like autistic children have.You don't think Jack has a problem do you?"

Henry put his arm round her. "He's a bit old for that to suddenly come out. Hormones more like, though it's a bit early for that. We'll keep an eye on him. I think he's just got really attuned to the wildlife and the silence and he didn't want it disturbed by something unnatural."

"So, wind chimes are hardly unnatural, they're like

what the Greeks had, an Aeolian Harp played by the wind? Well, maybe theirs weren't made in China for the mass market, "she conceded ruefully. "Maybe they are a bit naff."

"We've still got the box haven't we? We can give them to someone for Christmas."

Jack was a bit distant when he came down for supper but he made a subdued apology.

"I'm sorry I made such a fuss, I just got upset," was all the explanation they were going to get.

He couldn't begin to express the resentment he felt at the idea of those stupid chimes clanging below his bedroom window when he was trying to listen for the authentic notes of the elusive music he still sometimes heard drifting down from the Tump at night.

# Chapter 6

Jack's summer was full of activities. His new school friends helped clear undergrowth in the wood to build ramps for their mountain bikes and 'Uncle' George as the Freeman children now called him, oversaw the construction of a tree house in the biggest oak behind the house, accessed by a heavy wooden ladder dragged round from one of the barns. As time went on, this structure was destined to become more elaborate with a pitched roof wedged under one of the massive limbs of the tree, and a railing round the basic platform. There was only room for two children inside at a time, with a third sitting astride a sturdy branch and leaning in. The tree house provided a vantage point right opposite the end of the barn so they could see the barn owl chicks, now fledging, perched on the stone ledge of their nest site.

The adults took turns to climb up and look at them. Marie said they looked like the owls the children used to make at playschool out of toilet roll tubes and cotton wool, with brown paint smudges for feathers.

Chloe was only able to make use of the tree house with Jack when his friends were not around, which was not very often, and the girls who came to play didn't seem interested in contesting it.

Marie was delighted that Jack was so happily occupied, the only requirement being an unending supply of sandwiches, biscuits, crisps and squash. She was more concerned for Chloe though, since arranging play dates for her did not prove so easy. There were not many girls her age in the village and either their families seemed to have holiday plans or they already had 'best friends' and three often proved to be a crowd. The truth was, there was not as much to attract young girls to the farm as there was for boys.

There was a flurry of excitement however when the children found a small black cat living in the back of one of the sheds. She was very shy and at first was not prepared to let them get close, but they started leaving her food and gradually she became bolder. Samson and Delilah, the house cats who had taken readily to their new country life, avoided confrontation with the newcomer. They were brother and sister and as yet did not stray far from the house and farm yard.

The little feral cat was to be seen mousing along the hedgerows beyond the orchard however, but she regularly returned to her chosen spot among some sacks at the back of the open hay barn. Early one morning the children came running back in to report that there were kittens, just old enough to venture into the sunlight at the entrance, and when Henry and Marie came to investigate, there they were, six of them, all mixed colours, tumbling and playing, with their mother looking on.

The adults didn't go too close but the children gradually won their trust so that soon they could sit on the grass laughing, with kittens climbing all over them. This was an attraction for some of the local girls and Chloe was careful only to introduce them one at a time very quietly so that the mother cat wouldn't be disturbed and move her nest elsewhere.

In this way homes were found for four of the kittens while Jack and Chloe wore down their parents' resistance to keeping their two favourites, a ginger male they inevitably named Tom and a tortoiseshell female, her coat a splotch of black, chestnut and brown whom they called Fudge. Marie called the mother Jezebel, and since the children's old testament biblical knowledge was sketchy at best, they were happy with the name.

"She's going straight down to the vets when the kittens are weaned," Marie insisted, "and the kittens will have to be neutered as soon as they are old enough. Otherwise we'll be over run with cats."

"Another expense we could do without," she murmured outside of the children's hearing, "not to mention the food bill..."

The outside cats proved an asset though in one respect, they kept the mouse and rat population within bounds.

When Jack's friends came round and the boys rode their bikes up the well-worn path to the wood, Chloe would often trail along at a distance behind them, having nothing better to do. She knew they would not welcome her if she tried to join them, and in this instance Jack would be no support. Although he would have stood up for her if anyone had been mean, he knew his friends would regard his little sister as an nuisance and that would be an embarrassment.

She got into the habit of stopping at the field gate leading out onto the bridle path from the lane, waiting to see the riders who came by at intervals, often trotting or cantering past up the incline. Chloe was overcome by their magnificence. She was longing to ride, longing to stroke the horses necks and touch their soft noses.

One day an older lady came down at a walk and pulled her cob up to talk to Chloe who was breathless with excitement.

"Would you like to ride him down to the lane?" she asked, and dismounted to help Chloe into the saddle, rolling the stirrup leathers up to fit Chloe's short legs. What a delight!

"You hold the reins like this, you see? I'll walk in front. Don't worry, Charlie is very quiet, he'll just follow me."

And so Chloe had her first ride, never to be forgotten, and the start of a life-long involvement with horses. The lady let Chloe ride right down the lane past the farm gate and only lifted her down when they neared the big road.

" Oh, thank you so much!" Chloe's eyes were shining.

"You're very welcome," answered the lady, who had grandchildren of her own.

Chloe ran all the way home, almost colliding with her mother in the kitchen.

"You'll never guess what happened!"

At first Marie was concerned, immediately thinking it could easily have been any stranger who had lured her daughter away from the farm, and then,

"And you weren't wearing a hat?"

It was pretty irresponsible of this woman, however kindly she had meant it. Marie had no experience of horses but she knew the best of them could be unpredictable.

74

It was evident however that this was something Chloe really wanted to do. She had shown no interest in taking up ballet classes again although there was a dance school in the town.

So it was that a few days later Marie took Chloe round to the local riding school, not sure what kind of lessons were on offer or how much this new hobby was likely to cost. They arrived on a quiet afternoon and at first there did not seem to be anyone around except a boy in his late teens who was raking the arena with a ride-on mower dragging some sort of metal contraption that looked like a gate, and he ignored them completely. There were horses' heads looking out over the half doors of their loose boxes and Chloe went straight over to stroke their noses, including the one with a plaque on the door, reading, in very small type, 'Caution, this horse bites'. Luckily Marie did not see this warning and the horse must have been in a good mood; or perhaps it was a joke.

Marie was wondering what to do next when a blonde girl came out of the tack room and came over to speak to them.

"We do have children's lessons," she told Marie, "either in groups or one to one in the arena, and we do a children's hack some afternoons and Saturday Club when they can spend the day and ride as well as learning stable management. Pat is in the house, I'll call her to come and talk to you."

Pat Withenshaw was in her late forties, with the kind of no-nonsense air which many people found intimidating. She came striding out of the house and Marie found herself unconsciously straightening her back to return her firm  handshake.

"So this is your daughter?"

Pat lost no time on the evidently unhorsey mother, but turned to appraise the child. She had to keep several balls in the air to finance her own passion for horses; there were full liveries which were very lucrative, though the owners could be temperamental and needed some sweet talking at times, which did not come easily to Pat. She also took young horses to bring on or older horses someone else had soured or otherwise failed with, for reschooling, often competing them locally in the end to get the best price and make her commission by selling them to hopefully more suitable homes. Pat got on with horses better than she did people and this was the part of her work she really enjoyed.

Then there were the riding school ponies, all well behaved and well cared for. Insurance these days was astronomic for anything to do with teaching children to ride but it was an important part of her income and helped to keep the place afloat. Faced with yet another small pony mad girl, she pushed her fingers back through her short grey hair and observed the way Chloe was stroking the horses' noses, without poking them or startling them, and obviously unafraid .

Pat did not particularly like children, but once in a while a girl grew up to show real talent and if boyfriends did not get in the way at an early age, they might actually get somewhere, and these promising older pupils held her interest, though she was often disappointed as they went on to college and lost their competitive drive.

"Come and say hello to Miss Withenshaw," Marie

prompted, and Chloe came over obediently, instinctively wanting to make a good impression.

"So you want to learn to ride?" Pat asked.

It was surprising how often the child turned out to be less keen than the ambitious mother.

"Yes, I do, ever so much," Chloe said solemnly.

"Well why don't you come along at ten o'clock tomorrow and join the beginners class and if you take to it then maybe you can come for the day on Saturday. You can bring a packed lunch. You've met Rebecca already, she teaches most of the children's classes and leads the hacks,"Pat explained to Marie.

The weekly group lessons and Saturday Club were not as expensive as Marie had feared; if Chloe really liked it, then her Saturdays would be fully occupied with a shared lesson in the arena in the morning and a hack in the afternoon, with grooming and mucking out and cleaning tack  in between. It occurred to Marie that in a way this was free labour but no doubt it all took a lot of supervising, at least of the younger children.

"What about riding clothes?" she thought to ask.

"We can lend her a hat to start with, though if she comes regularly you'll need to buy one. She can come in jeans and wear trainers at first but I have a trunk full of second hand jods and boots which I sell to raise money for  SPANA, the  horse charity. So it needn't be a big investment," Pat assured her, rightly assessing this was not one of those well-heeled mothers for whom money was no object. And so Marie had to find time to run Chloe over to the stables and pick her up again, but it was worth it to see her daughter so happy.

Marie's parents came to stay for a few days and that was a pleasant interlude. Her mother kept her reservations to herself now, knowing the die was cast and they had to make the best of it. Their grand- parents took Jack and Chloe to the beach, which Henry and Marie had not had time to do, although it was only a few miles away. Watching the children running down to the sea to fill their buckets and build sand castles, their grandmother said,

" It's a pity Marie doesn't have time to take them out much, this is really no distance at all."

They sat on a rock with a flask of coffee, keeping an eye on the children. The tide was in and a light breeze got up as it started to turn, gulls swooped and wheeled against the blue sky and they heard the faint whistle of the steam train making its way along the track with the backdrop of wooded hills behind.

"You can see why Henry's grand- parents ended up down here," they agreed. " If they make a go of things, maybe we should think about it."

They still had serious doubts about the future, but putting their worries to one side, they concentrated on enjoying this precious time with the children whom they were now able to see so rarely.

"I expect they're getting hungry, let's get some fish and chips and an ice cream. Come on kids, time for some food."

Towelling the children down and helping them pull on tee shirts and shorts, their grandma gave them a hug. 'They're happy enough,' she thought, 'and it's all an experience for them I suppose.'

Back at the cottage, Marie's mother asked where the spinning wheel and small loom were, which she used to be so keen to use. Marie had to admit she had no time for crafts at the moment.

"I have been into the craft shop in town a few times now and I do want to follow up on that. There's another mother at the school who does textile panels and felting, and I've spoken to her a bit. There doesn't seem to be a local gallery to exhibit craft work, though there are a few fairs during the summer where people set up stalls. It would be great if there was a permanent space where people could exhibit though, I'm sure there's plenty of talent around. To be honest I even thought of using the big barn where Henry has his office as a workshop and display other people's work for sale on commission. It'd be quite a tie because it would have to be open regular hours, but I'm around most of the time anyway. I think I'll look into that in the autumn when we're a bit less busy just getting the place straight."

Her mother encouraged the idea, not that she thought it would bring in very much money but everything helped. She was worried to see how hard Marie was working though. The arrival of the hens was another commitment, though they seemed not to take too much looking after, and already they were laying. Local people quickly showed an interest, genuine free range eggs were popular, and the owners of the deli took what was left. Even the gastro pub was keen to put local eggs on the menu and Marie could see that side of their business expanding.

One morning when Marie dropped Chloe off at the stables she decided to stay to watch, leaning on the railing of the arena, to see how she was getting on. Chloe was confident and loved the feel of being in the saddle so already she was able to rise to trot and maintain her balance without hauling on the reins for support. Marie was quite impressed with her progress, but of course she was no judge. She did not notice that someone had approached her until the woman spoke.

"Is that your daughter on the skewbald pony? I thought I recognised her. I think your son is in my daughter's class at school, Jack is it?"

"Yes, that's right." Marie knew her now, she always looked immaculate at pick up time, as if she spent all day in designer slacks and silk shirts with pie crust collars, which in fact she probably did. Lucinda and her husband were architects she seemed to remember, from what Marie had gathered at the school gates.

Apart from saying hello she didn't seem to have anything to say to the other mothers, and the feeling was obviously mutual. It didn't help that word had got round that her daughter Tamsin would be going to a private school in a year's time, rather than the comprehensive like everyone else.

'I must say,' Marie thought when she heard this, 'It'd take a lot to get me to put an 11 year old on a bus at 7.15 every morning however much money we had. They don't get back 'til six thirty and even go in on Saturday mornings. Still, they get longer holidays, I suppose that makes up for it a bit.'

Lucinda was being very friendly now however, praising Chloe's seat and the way she held her reins. She was dressed for riding herself and pointed out Tamsin who had brought her own pretty grey welsh

80

pony round from the row of loose boxes where the private liveries were stabled.

Tamsin started to groom the pony which nuzzled her arm and Marie noticed how well they seemed to get on together.

"Tamsin loves that pony, and in many ways they've been the perfect combination," Lucinda told her. " They've done so well at shows and pony club activities, but she's really outgrown Tinkerbell and we're looking out for a bigger pony for her. Pat has found something suitable and Tamsin has ridden him a couple of times but she's in tears if we even mention parting with Tink so we have a stalemate at the moment. I keep my own horse here and frankly two liveries to pay for is quite enough."

Marie agreed that 'paying to keep a pony they didn't use made no sense but if Tamsin was going to be heartbroken, it was a problem.' Lucinda then made an admission.

"I'm really glad I bumped into you," she said.

Marie began to wonder how accidental that had been when she went on,

"Am I right in thinking you've taken over a farm?"

"Quite a small one," Marie told her.

"Yes, well I was just wondering whether you might consider renting out a field for the ponies? It wouldn't have to be very big because they can't have too much grass in case they get laminitis. Of course if there was a field shelter, it would be even better. I know I've rather sprung this on you, but what do you think? The thing is, Chloe could ride Tinkerbell and come out hacking with us. I can easily ride over to you from here...."

She had obviously got it all worked out.

Marie was taken aback by this suggestion. It had never occurred to them to involve anyone else on the farm and they certainly didn't want to take on any more responsibility.

"I really don't know," she said. "I would have to discuss it with my husband. We haven't time to look after any more animals that's for sure."

It would be some regular extra income though, she thought, and when Chloe had learned to ride properly it would save paying for her to ride at the stables. That would have to be part of the deal.

"Oh No, we would look after the ponies. If they lived out, with maybe access to some shelter, we would just need to feed them really."

Lucinda was seeking to reassure her, but Marie suspected there would be times when they had to get involved, if it was only to give them hay and what about mucking out their shelter, whatever form that took. They would have to be firm and stick to whatever was agreed. It was worth considering though.

"Well if you give me your number, we'll talk it over. We'll have to think whether there is some pasture we can spare and what stabling we could provide."

Already she was wondering whether the disused calf shed might be suitable, there was a small field attached to that which they didn't really need for the sheep, although she had wondered about keeping a few goats there.

Marie wanted to discuss the potential grass livery with Henry as soon as she got home, but he had news of his own.

"George says there's a farm sale over at North Molton

on Friday. There's a trailer in the catalogue which should be good to go with the Fergie. We'll need something to haul the hay when we cut it and you can't expect to borrow one this time of year. We were going to have to buy one eventually."

He'd promised George a pub lunch and was evidently excited at the thought of a day out.

"So if you buy it, how are you going to get it home?' she asked. "You aren't going to drive the tractor all that way to pick it up?"

"Well, hardly," he laughed at the idea of trundling 20 miles in the old Fergie with a queue of furious holiday makers building up behind, even supposing it was up to the journey.

"I can tow it behind the Volvo ;we've never used the tow bar but I don't see why not. Well, so long as I don't have to do any reversing anyway."

Once that was settled, Marie told him about Lucinda's idea of keeping the ponies at Holtbourne. They agreed to ask George what he thought, he might have some idea what rent they could charge.George had a typical farmer's attitude to horses; he wasn't keen, they kicked up the ground and needed more acreage than sheep. Given that they needed an income however, he thought it was not unreasonable to ask £25 a week per horse if they were providing some shelter as well. This sounded like a useful contribution to their mounting expenses and since these were ponies not large horses and Chloe was to be allowed to ride, they decided to include hay as they were likely to get a good crop. Lucinda was delighted and it was agreed that the ponies should move over as soon as the new pony arrived.

On Friday evening the Volvo arrived back in the yard towing a flat bed trailer. Henry and George were in high spirits after a change of scene and pleased with their purchases, including a chainsaw which later proved to be rather temperamental, an old set of Lister clippers for shearing and some baler twine which they would need for haymaking. They also spent all of £3 on a wooden box full of bits and pieces. The out of date medicines would have to be thrown out but there was a ram harness and raddle and some other things Henry couldn't identify.

Seeing how happy he was after a day out, Marie felt guilty, realising that her life was more varied than Henry's who was splitting his time between work on the land and out buildings and trying to focus on his old job which was still their only source of income.

" When things settle down a bit," she told him later, " I want you to have more time for yourself, otherwise you'll burn out."

"I'm alright," he reassured her. "It's all coming together now. You'll see, it'll calm down as we get into the autumn. We've only been here a couple of months and look what we've achieved."

It was true, their hard work was paying off ;their home was beginning to look like any other Exmoor farm, and in some ways tidier since Henry had got rid of the many pieces of baler twine that he found supporting sagging fences or tying gates closed.

"I think the whole of Exmoor is held together by baler twine," he joked.

They were beginning to feel proud to show callers

around.

With a spell of settled dry weather, George urged Henry to take in the hay.

"You don't want it all to go to seed," he said. "If we cut it tomorrow, with this heat we can turn it in a couple of days, give it another day or so and bale the following day when the sun is well up and the dew is off."

Henry was keen to get this important job out of the way. George enjoyed driving the tractor and was of course much better at cutting straight swathes and turning at the end of the rows, but Henry took turns and was pleased when George congratulated him on doing a 'proper job.' Turning the hay was easy and as the weather held it dried well. Henry was delighted as the baler steadily deposited bale after bale of hay around the fields.

"I'm amazed at how much we've got!" he said to George.

"Oh yes, you've got a fair crop there," he replied. "At best you can get 80 bales an acre but nothing's been done to the fields early in the year, so you won't get that kind of yield. Still you'll get plenty for your needs and the ponies, and you'll have some to sell after Christmas if you don't get through it too quick. Those horse women are always looking for extra at the end of the winter and you can get £4.50 a bale for it then."

They had managed well on their own so far, but hauling it all into the yard was a job that required help. On a larger farm there would have been a second tractor but they were having to do it the hard way. George was on the tractor, being the least physical job, although

Henry was worried that after a hard week his old friend was getting tired. There was no doubt George was in his element though, directing operations. They were having to keep uncoupling the trailer to drive the tractor round the field lifting each bale on prongs to deposit it on the trailer and then recoupling to bring the loads into the yard.

At Marie's suggestion Henry had offered to pay Johnny who helped out at the stables to provide some muscle and they roped in Thomas's sons Ryan and Sean together with three of Jack's mountain biking friends to lend a hand.

Henry had promised to take the boys to see the latest blockbuster movie with a burger afterwards by way of reward. Thomas's sons knew enough to make sure the bales were stacked in alternate layers, side on and end on for stability and the younger lads took turns hauling the bales in the barn. Henry worked with George while Johnny unloaded the trailer as it came in and supervised the lads.

It took the whole day back and forth before all the hay was safely stored. Marie had provided endless refreshments including ice lollies and cornets, and the boys went home happy. They were tired and grubby, but it had been a laugh and they had taken time out to lark about. Henry paid Johnny a bit extra and thanked him sincerely. He had worked hard all day, organising the boys and keeping them on track which came better from him than from either of the men.

At last Henry and George were left alone in the yard sitting with a beer and looking at the Linhay Barn which was stacked full from floor to roof.

"That's a good job done," Henry said.

" It's good sweet hay too," George replied, "You can smell it from here . I've missed that since I gave up farming."

"I honestly don't think we'd have got the place off the ground without you George. I had no idea what was involved when we took it on."

"It cuts both ways you know," George replied. "It means a lot to me coming up here. When Mavis passed away the bungalow was just a shell. She'd always be busy about the place, you know, cooking and knitting and telling me the gossip. I kept the garden up but my heart wasn't in it, and when I went into the pub I had nothing to say to people, I was turning into an old man. Now I'm in the thick of it again, there's things to be getting on with and your missus is so kind and the kiddies rope me in with their bikes and the big swing. That little maid of yours calls me 'Uncle George.' I feel like I'm part of something again."

"You're part of the family now George, you know that don't you?" Henry helped him to his feet. "Are you coming in for some supper?"

"I won't if you don't mind.  To be honest I'm a bit too tired for company tonight. I've got some ham and cheese at home, that'll do me, I've been well fed these past few days."

"Well, let me give you a lift down the road then."
Henry was feeling guilty, exhaustion had caught up with George now he had stopped working.

"No, no, it's but a step down the lane, I'll be alright. That was a good job done, I'm pleased. See you tomorrow maybe," He waved as he walked off through the gate, making an effort to be jaunty until he had turned the corner into the lane.

"I should have noticed how tired he was getting, there's no shelter from the sun with no cab on the tractor and that seat is hard even with a cushion on it. I feel bad about it now," Henry told Marie.

"Oh, poor old George, he did look worn out by the end. We'll go round tomorrow and check on him," she replied. "Still, you know he wouldn't have missed it for the world."

"I know," Henry replied "But I don't want to take advantage of his good nature."

Lucinda was anxious that the livery worked out well and at first she drove over every day, although as time went on Tamsin cycled round and if she was bossy and showed off a bit, Chloe didn't mind, she was quick to learn and loved being around the horses. Henry had removed some partitions from the calf pens to make an open shelter for the ponies.

"I can feed them and give them their hay in the winter and put their warm rugs on," Chloe told her mother.

"We'll see about that, I don't want you doing all the work." Marie was not going to have her little daughter exploited.

Lucinda kept her promise to take Chloe riding however and most weekends they went up the bridle path beside the farm and out onto the open moor where there were tracks leading off in several directions. Chloe was delighted.

"We ride past the gate where I used to wait to see the

horses, and now I'm the one riding," she told Marie.

# Chapter 7

One afternoon Lucinda led the girls along a shortcut which brought them within sight of a dilapidated caravan, fenced off to form a piece of rough garden with a vegetable patch and a few hens scratching. An older woman appeared in the open doorway, watching them as they passed. In her faded raincoat and gum boots she took up a challenging stance, although Lucinda called out a deliberately cheerful greeting,

"Hello Dr. Laidlaw, lovely day isn't it?"

There was no response however, the shaggy grey head and lined features might have been made of stone.

"Who was that?" Chloe asked when they were safely past, "Is she really a doctor?"

"Not the kind you're thinking of," Lucinda told her. "She was a university lecturer at one time, I believe she taught history. She's very keen on local folklore, that sort of thing, she even wrote a book about it; I think your farm is mentioned, or at least the history of the Hall."

"Is she allowed to live in that caravan? Doesn't she need planning permission?"

Tamsin knew all about it, this was a subject she often heard her parents discuss.

"Strictly speaking, she probably does," her mother replied, " But she seems to be occupying the furthest corner of land belonging to the Hall and no-one has ever disputed it."

When they got back into the yard, Marie was coming out of the orchard having locked the hens up for the night.

"We saw a funny lady," Chloe told her, "She was quite scary."

Marie looked to Lucinda for enlightenment and as the girls were untacking the ponies Lucinda told her what she knew about Lilian Laidlaw.

"She was quite a brilliant scholar apparently and could have been a professor if she wasn't so cantankerous. Eventually she fell out with the faculty and retired down here. At first she moved into the Hall; she'd known Anthony Sinclair's father rather well, there's talk of them having an affair donkey's years ago. Anyway she ended up moving into the caravan. I guess she's harmless enough, just rather eccentric, but she does go around with a shotgun a lot of the time which is a bit off-putting."

The Freeman children had another encounter with their unfriendly neighbour not long after. One weekend, Lucinda entered Tamsin and the new pony Rowan at a local show. Chloe didn't want to miss out on riding and badgered to be allowed to hack out on her own.

"Absolutely not," her parents objected. "It doesn't matter how quiet the pony is, you're far too young to go out on your own."

Naturally, this led to tears and finally Jack, who had nothing better to do, suggested he walk up onto the hill with Chloe on the pony to see that she came to no harm. He could take Taffy and give her a good run while he was at it. Chloe agreed to stay in walk so he could keep up and ran upstairs to get into her jodhpurs.

"Now you won't let her out of your sight,will you?" their parents insisted and he promised he wouldn't. Needless to say, by the time they emerged from the bridle path onto the open moor, Jack was slightly out of breath and Chloe was itching to "just trot on round the hill and come straight back down."

"Don't go right out on top then," he told her, "Come back down the shortcut."

Making his way over the heather towards the path he expected Chloe to descend, Jack came suddenly upon the caravan, which he hadn't seen before. Taffy was running ahead chasing a rabbit and by the time he caught up with her he found a frightening situation unfolding with some mad old woman pointing a shot gun at his dog.

"Don't you dare shoot my dog. What do you think you're doing?"

He came running forward, calling, "Heel Taffy!"

The collie turned back to him obediently while he glared angrily at the wild looking figure confronting him. To give her her due, she did lower the gun, looking around for other intruders.

"Where are the rest of you?" she demanded.

"What do you mean, I'm on my own," he told her, puzzled now rather than alarmed.

"If you're out hiking you'd better catch up with the others, the track's that way," she pointed.

"I told you, I'm on my own, I'm not a grockle. We live down there at Holtbourne."

"Oh, I heard the farm had been sold. So you're the new family?"

"Yes, and I've got every right to be up here with my

92

dog without being threatened with a gun."

Jack didn't usually talk to adults this way but he was still indignant, and anyway, there was something so direct about this woman it was almost childlike. Meeting each other's gaze there was a moment of subliminal recognition, unlikely kindred spirits. Lilian leaned the gun against the caravan and said,

"You get gangs of grockles up here in the summer, wandering about with no respect for the countryside or anything in it, shouting, dogs barking and disturbing the wildlife."

"I'm sure that's true,"Jack agreed with her. "Gang doesn't quite describe them though, more like a gaggle milling about."

"Now that's a very good collective noun," she chuckled. "A Gaggle of Grockles, I like that."

At this point Chloe appeared, coming over the brow of the hill on Tink.

"That's my sister," he told her hurriedly, in case she should take umbrage again. "I'm supposed to be taking care of her."

"You're not doing a very good job of it then are you? I've seen her before with that woman on her thoroughbred and the girl on the fancy pony."

Chloe came on down to join them, and following behind came a group of Exmoor ponies. Luckily the ponies stopped on the hillside, their attention caught by something the humans could not see.

"Oh, they've given up." Chloe was relieved, "Sometimes they follow us all the way down to the hunting gate and crowd round us on the path. They're looking at something else now."

"They can stand like that for ages," Lilian said. "I think they are listening to Pan's pipes."

"Is that what it is? Really?" Jack asked urgently.

Lilian was struck by his tone and turned to look at him intently. An unusual boy, she realised, with his thick head of bronze curls which caught the sunlight, high cheekbones and almond eyes. He would never be conventionally handsome, but his intensity and charisma were attractive. Slim and wiry he seemed almost to stand on tiptoe, as if about to spring into action, something goat like.

'If I were inclined to believe in astrology,' she thought, 'I'd say he must be Capricorn.'

She regarded him in silence for a moment before deciding to speak. "You've heard it then?"

He was defensive now. "Why, have you?"
"I think I hear the music drifting up from down there," she indicated the direction of the farm, and then, "Gerard Sinclair knew all about it."
"Does he live round here?"
"Oh, he died long ago." Jack was disappointed.

Marie had not been too preoccupied to keep in contact with Sally, but it was rather a one sided communication. Sally didn't always answer the phone and then she was guarded, even when Matthew was not at home. She asked about the farm, even sounding a bit envious hearing about Marie's new life in the village but all she would say about herself was that things were 'alright' and that she had plenty of translating work to do. Then suddenly Sally called briefly and said,

"I've got a new phone, so please don't contact me on

the old one."

She gave Marie a different number and then she said,

"I'm going off social media for a while, and please don't give anyone at all the new number, alright?"

"Yes, of course," Marie was trying to weigh up the implications. "So you've cancelled the old contract?" thinking, 'But that doesn't mean she has to change her number.'

"Are you still at the flat?"

"Yes, of course, look I have to go now. Thanks Marie," and the line went dead.

Marie came to the conclusion that Sally was keeping this phone from Matthew, so his surveillance must be getting heavier.

'I hope he doesn't find this one or he will really think she has something to hide.'

Marie was worried that things could turn nasty. She felt like calling the new number and warning Sally to leave now before the situation got out of hand, but in the end she just sent a non-committal text asking her to keep in touch and saying,

"You know I'm always here for you."

She had a sense of foreboding though and it preyed on her mind.


Marie had not had time to make any close friends in the village and when Ellie arrived on the doorstep with a suggestion that she join the women's skittle team at The Plough when they started playing again in the autumn, she was tempted. As she got to know Ellie better, Marie was more at ease in her company and she asked her in for a coffee.

"I'll have a think about it," she promised. "Henry sometimes has to do office work in the evenings and I don't like to abandon the kids, but it sounds like a good way to meet some other women, real locals if you know what I mean."

"Oh yeah, I went to school with most of them," Ellie told her. "It's a laugh and it's a chance to get out of the house and away from the men for an evening."

"That sounds a bit heart felt," Marie smiled, sensing an undertone here.

"Oh, I've just been having words with Thomas, he can be a bit hard on the boys sometimes."

Marie reached over and drew the kettle back onto the hotplate of the Aga.

"More coffee?" she asked, sensing Ellie was in the mood to share her grievances. She added some chocolate biscuits to the plate between them on the big pine kitchen table; you couldn't have too much chocolate at moments like these.

"Yes, thanks Marie, I'm in no hurry to get back to be honest. Thomas is a good father, don't get me wrong and the boys do need a firm hand but sometimes he can be a bit too much like his own father for my liking."

Marie was puzzled, Henry had always thought well of Cliff as far as she could gather.

"It was the way he was brought up himself I suppose, life was harder in those days. It wasn't a big thing, it's just his attitude and the way he speaks to them. Ryan wanted to go off with a friend so Sean didn't see why he should help to move the stock on his own. Thomas had a go at them and it just reminded me of the old man. Thomas was tough, he was a big lad and could hold his own so I suppose he's right when he says it never did him any harm, but Josh was younger and more sensitive and from what his mother told me, Cliff was always picking on him, he couldn't do anything right or work hard enough to please his father. She said Cliff was trying to get some reaction from Josh, he'd have respected him more if he'd shouted back like Thomas, but instead Josh just went in on himself. I sometimes think that's why Josh has never had a serious relationship. Plenty of girls have been interested and he has had relationships but he never commits to anyone; it's as if he isn't in touch with his feelings and I don't want that to happen to our boys."

"But he seems quite outgoing; he doesn't talk a lot but he's friendly."

Marie knew Josh played the guitar when the pub held Folk evenings, he seemed confident socially.

"Yes, he'd do anything for anyone, but he never talks about what's going on inside and that's not healthy."

"You don't think he's depressed, do you?" Marie asked. "People can be good at hiding that," suddenly she thought of Sally again.

"What makes you say that?" Ellie asked sharply. "Have you noticed something?"

"Oh No, sorry, I was just reminded of a friend of mine. She's in an awful abusive relationship and she doesn't seem to have the will to get out of it."

"A lot of farmers get isolated and end up committing suicide," Ellie told her, "But Josh is nothing like that. As for your friend, I can never understand how women put up with that. Even if you have kids and no job there's always a way out."

Ellie was obviously critical of anyone less strong minded than herself.

"Well, I'd better get back and get some food on the go," she put on her jacket." Thanks for the coffee and chat, we should do it more often."

Marie wasn't sure she meant that sincerely, and was suddenly uncomfortable, feeling she and Ellie didn't have that much in common after all. She was left thinking the village skittles team might not be quite what she was looking for. As she stepped out into the yard to wave Ellie off, Marie noticed dark clouds gathering in the west, the direction of the prevailing wind.

"The weather's breaking," Ellie said as she started the land rover, "Lucky we got the crops in, though the yield's down with all that dry weather early on."

That night the family were woken by a spectacular storm with sheet lightening and rumbles in the distance building to crashing thunderclaps overhead. Jack loved it, watching from his attic window as the Tump was lit dramatically by the flashes, but Chloe crept into her parents' bed where they distracted her with Norse myths about Thor's hammer and and his chariot crossing the sky.

That was the end of the settled weather and already there was a feeling of autumn in the air. On fine days there was a heavy heat and they hurried to get the fruit picked from the orchard before it started to rot. The trees had not been pruned but there was far more than the family could eat. They didn't expect to be able to sell the apples, everyone locally seemed to have a glut of those, but the shop took some of the pears and plums. There was even a damson tree and a greengage which were fiddly to prepare because of the stones, but Marie made jam to sell along with the eggs. She had left a notice by the gate asking for jam jars, so now she was able to add to the small income stream from their produce. Stirring the pan was hot work and sterilizing and filling the jars was time consuming but the children were back in school and she enjoyed it.

The farm house faced south and they had enjoyed some lovely dawns and sunsets during the summer. Now, in the fading September heat, showers and sunshine combined to create the rainbows which are such a feature of Exmoor.

One afternoon the family were standing in the back porch dodging a sudden downpour when Jack pointed, "Look a double rainbow. "

They stood watching as the colours filled the arc of the sky and then gradually faded.

"It'll soon be autumn," Marie told the children. "The swallows are gathering on the wires waiting for the next steady westerly wind to begin their long migration to Africa. They'll be back again next year, repairing the same nests though."

"I think it's sad they have to go away every year," Chloe said. "They're safe here, some of them may not come back."

"That's true darling, but the trees are already beginning to turn and the nights are drawing in now, and they don't mind going, it's in their nature," Marie hugged her tender-hearted daughter.

"We can enjoy each season as it comes," Henry told them.

In the evenings he had been pointing out the winter constellations as they appeared in the Southern sky, Orion with his belt directly in front of the house, with Pleiades, the seven sisters, to the right, and Cassiopea and the Plough further to the West. Jupiter and Venus had been bright and he was trying to teach the children about the phases of the moon.

"We're so lucky here," he told them, "Exmoor is an official Dark Skies area, there's no light pollution and people come from the towns to see the stars. Next time the rangers lay on a night walk we'll go along shall we?" Jack was particularly keen on that idea.

Word got round at The Plough that the Freemans wanted an Exmoor ram to serve their ewes. They didn't want to buy one for such a small flock and Henry had taken on board Thomas's remark that they might be able to borrow an older animal which was coming to the end of his breeding days, but it seemed a cheek to ask.

When he went in for a well earned pint one early evening, after a hard day of Team meetings online, he was approached by an older man he recognised.

Bert was always scruffy, with a tweed jacket that had seen better days and a greasy cap. He was said to graze sheep on every bit of land he could scrounge and even sometimes on the broad drover's verges along quieter lanes; one of the traditional village characters who were gradually dying out.

"Hear you're looking for a ram."
He nudged his empty glass in Henry's direction, who took the hint and ordered a pint of Exmoor Gold.

"I've got a good old 'un would do you, he's sired some

lovely lambs in his time. Nice and quiet he is too."

Henry agreed that this paragon among sheep might be what he needed, though they were not going to put a ram in with the flock until November to avoid lambing in the worst of the winter weather.

"Thing is, I like to make a bit of cider," Bert continued, "And you've got a good orchard over at your place so I expect you've a lot of apples and pears going to waste."

"We do have more than we need," Henry conceded.

"Well if you want to bring me over a trailer load of good fruit, not too bruised and no rotten ones mind, and let's say 20 bales of hay, you can have Basil for nothing."

While it was not quite 'nothing' this was all produce Henry had to spare. He suggested coming over with George to see the ram, not trusting himself to spot any obvious defects in the animal. Besides, George knew everyone and would tell him if Bert was likely to be passing on something that was no longer up to the job.

"If you give me your number I'll call you," Henry suggested.

"I don't bother with mobile phones and such, George Binnicombe knows where to find me."

Bert downed the last of his pint and wandered off, since Henry, not wanting to look like a soft touch, did not offer to refill it.

A few days later George and Henry parked the Volvo outside a ramshackle cottage. They wove a path through the front garden which was cluttered with derelict vehicles and made their way round to the back where Bert was leaning on a gate smoking a roll up.

"There you are then," he greeted them as if they had

come by arrangement. "Come on," and they followed him over to a pen where two massive Exmoor rams stood companionably together. They looked much the same to Henry; he wasn't sure which he was supposed to be considering so he was relieved when George enlightened him by pointing out the younger animal, saying,

"This is your new tup then. He looks like a useful sort."

"He is," Bert agreed, " I gave good money for him. Mind you, he'd have you over in a trice, you'd not turn your back on him."

Looking at the massive curling horns on both powerful animals, now he could see them up close, Henry had a moment's doubt about handling a ram, clearly a very different proposition to their docile ewes. Bert assured them however that Basil had a very different temperament; even when he was younger he had never been aggressive, and as if to prove it, the old ram came over to the fence and stuck his nose through the bars, inviting Henry to scratch his woolly poll.

"He'll do you alright," was George's verdict.

On the way home he reminded Henry that the ram could only serve the flock for two years until his daughters were ready to breed, after that he would probably have to 'go on' as he put it, being too old by then to pass on to anyone else. Henry knew his family had not yet come to terms with sending male sheep to market where they would be bought for slaughter.

They had to be practical, but he suspected rightly that anything individual with a name would be hard to part with. Basil wouldn't cost a lot to keep but it was something else to be cared for; still, if he was as friendly as he seemed, he was probably destined to live to a ripe old age.

When Bert brought their new addition over a few days later, they agreed with Lucinda to put him in with the ponies for company. They kept a strict eye on him at first but they seemed to get on; they were grazing one of the lower fields which had been mown for hay and new grass had come through so the animals wandered up and down the field contentedly together.

Hannah was one of Marie's regular customers. Dressed in brightly coloured skirts or harem pants and with a long brown plait to her waist she was a distinctive figure; she had first told Marie about the craft shop in town when they met at the school gates.

One morning she brought a friend over to buy eggs, a tall young woman with blonde dreadlocks whom she introduced as Sophie. They stayed chatting at the gate and Sophie said,

"Actually we're neighbours you know. Hannah and I both live at the Hall."

"Really?" Marie had been curious to know what went on there.

"You should come and see us, you're interested in crafts aren't you? We've got some great workshops, Sophie does jewellery, there's a glass blower and a forge. Jed does some amazing wrought iron work, and I make clothing as well as the felting," Hannah told her.

Marie went round the following day and was given a tour.

"It's fascinating," she told Henry afterwards. "The

house is quite Arts and Crafts, with lots of carved panelling and tapestries, but really run down. I didn't meet Anthony but the girls showed me round, big rooms with threadbare carpets, full of antique furniture which might be worth a fortune and some of Gerard Sinclair's pictures. There's a library with thousands of books. You should come and see, they've invited us to a Barbecue so we can take the kids."

They duly turned up on Saturday afternoon, bringing red wine and brownies as a contribution and were soon talking to the other residents and crafts people who were sitting on a broad terrace where grass grew through the cracked paving, but somehow the overgrown garden and broken stone fountain added an old world charm to the scene. Jack and Chloe came back from exploring the garden and dragged Henry off to see the pond, rank with weed, where large golden carp were gliding in the green water, and Marie found herself sitting next to Hannah.

They started to talk about fabric and Hannah told her she had a source of imported cloth from Jaipur which explained the vibrant deep blues, reds and gold of the garments she made, all traditional colours of Rajasthan.

"But you told me you do weaving, didn't you?" Hannah asked.

"Yes, mostly wool, and I spin, that's why I'm so excited to be keeping my own sheep," Marie replied. "My loom can weave weft up to ninety centimetres. I'm really keen to get into it properly. I want to experiment with natural dyes too."

Hannah was impressed.

"I'm sure there must be a demand for cloth like that, in fact I would love to make cloaks out of it, but it's not as easy as you might think to sell craft work round here. The locals aren't really interested and we've never managed to tap into the tourist market. We're off the beaten track and Anthony won't let us advertise, he doesn't want strangers on the property."

Marie had gathered that from the prohibition he had put on selling the farm via the internet.

"I'd been wondering about setting up a craft centre in our big barn," Marie told her.

"Wow, that's a fabulous idea!" Hannah was enthusiastic. "I'm sure we'd all like to get involved with that."

"Maybe we could have a meeting here then and see who's up for it," Marie was encouraged. "I could get it set up in the winter and we could publicise it online and through the Tourist Information Centre in the Spring."

They agreed that Hannah and Sophie would run the idea past the other crafts people.

# Chapter 8

Marie received a puzzling text from Sally, again with no explanation. It read:

'Hi Marie, I've got a favour to ask. Please can you message the old number as if you haven't heard from me for a while and are kind of giving up contacting me. Sorry to ask, but please do it today.'

Marie realised this was for Matthew's benefit, who was obviously monitoring Sally's phone, but how to word it to sound genuine? Finally she texted:

'Hi Sally, I guess you're busy. Hope things are going well with you. It's been pretty full on all summer down here and I don't see myself getting back in your direction this year. Maybe if I come up some time I'll give you a ring. Vaya con Dios, Marie.'

That sounded dismissive enough she hoped.
That weekend Sally phoned, overwrought and almost incoherent.

"I'm really sorry to ask, but can I come down for a few days? I've got to get away and I can't think of anywhere else he won't find me."

No need for Marie to ask who she was frightened of.

"Yes, of course, where are you?"

"I'm in Reading, there's a train to Taunton in a couple of hours, is there a bus I can take over to you?"

The answer to that was in the negative.

"Just let me know which train you're on and I'll pick you up," Marie assured her. "The train comes in to the back of the station so come straight out from the platform and I'll meet you there."

She went to tell Henry about their unexpected guest. He had only met Sally on a couple of occasions and a distraught woman landing herself on them was hardly ideal but he remembered what Marie had told him in the spring and took it with good grace.

"I'll get some bolognaise out to defrost," Marie was getting organised, "And make the chicken pie tomorrow."

"Alright, don't worry, I'll hold the fort here," he gave her a hug. 'Marie to the rescue as usual,' he thought. "Drive carefully for Heaven's sake."

The train was on time for once and as Sally came through the barrier, lugging two large cases, Marie was struck by how haggard she looked. Not only was she even thinner than in the spring, but her face was white and gaunt and her blue eyes had a hunted look as she glanced around. Only the luxuriant chestnut hair was the same, curling down as if it had a life of its own. Once in the car the floodgates opened and Sally at last poured out the whole story.

"You saw what it was like before you left," she said. "Matthew just got worse, more suspicious, more possessive. He followed me to the hairdressers once, then when I caught him looking at my phone and I asked him what he was doing, he threw it across the floor and broke the screen. I took it to get it repaired and the guy had to fiddle with it to get it to work so he noticed there was a hidden tracker app on it. Matthew had been stalking me, God knows for how long, spying on my every move. I felt sick when he told me. That was when

I bought the second phone. I kept it turned off and hid it in the spools compartment in the body of the sewing machine. I got really paranoid then and felt I was being watched all the time. I still don't know if he set up hidden cameras in the flat. I wouldn't put it past him."

"Poor you," Marie was horrified. "So that was when you left him?"

"I spent days trying to make a plan, thinking of all the things I would have to do. And I had nowhere set up to go. I got the agency to pay my translation fees into a new bank account. I had to tell him they were late paying that month because of course he noticed it had not gone through. I didn't have a personal account because before things got too bad, Matthew had got me to put my salary into a joint account for the rent and everything because he was sensitive about me earning more than him. I think sometimes that was the beginning of the problem really, that he felt I was belittling him and had more financial power in the relationship."

"He's just a snake through and through," Marie told her. "I bet if you talked to his ex girlfriend she would tell the same story."

"It's funny you say that, I have been wondering. He was always telling me what a mean bitch she was and how she walked out for no reason but I think that's what he would say about me now."

"You've left him now, that's the main thing," Marie was trying to calm her down but Sally was in full flow and Marie did want to understand the whole situation, since she was now involving her family by taking Sally in.

"Then one of the guys from the agency came round

on his way home at five minutes notice to discuss some edits to a translation. Matthew walked in and just hit the roof. Stephen was really shocked and left pretty quickly but Matthew went ballistic, refusing even to look at the amendments I tried to show him, accusing me of having an affair. Stephen is fifty years old and gay for Heaven's sake, but Matthew wasn't listening. Finally he hit me and I fell against the fireplace, there was blood everywhere.Then he stormed out and I just packed and left. End of. I turned up on my mother's doorstep late that night, which wasn't fair to her and after I'd told her everything we made a list of things I had to do. I gave notice on the flat, luckily it only had to be one month because we were out of the six month initial contract and I told the agent in no uncertain terms that I was giving up my half of the joint tenancy so it was up to them if they let Matthew stay. He said that would have to be a new single tenancy and he would email Matthew and ask him if he wanted to apply for that. I know he won't be able to afford the rent on his own but that's not my problem is it?"

"Absolutely not!" Marie assured her indignantly.

"I had trouble accessing the joint bank account on line because Matthew kept changing the passwords. I knew that would be a problem but luckily it was with one of the high street banks and I made an appointment and managed to get some money out of it. There wasn't as much as I expected in there, but that's probably no surprise. I told them I wanted to take my name off it but they said they'd have to close it to do that. I did manage to cancel any overdraft facility on it anyway and luckily it was in credit because I had kept paying in. I know

Matthew has a credit card and I know he used to pay the minimum off that out of that account so he'll have to sort that out. Anyway, I think they will close the joint account, they seemed to be used to people splitting up."

"I bet they are," said Marie.

"The agency will still send me work when I want it, they're glad to have me. I was only at Mum's flat for three days before Matthew gave up calling and tracked me down there. I'd been planning to get myself a flat somewhere, but I didn't have time to plan that far ahead. He turned up on the doorstep last night, she has a ground floor flat in a mansion block and he started banging on the door and swearing when I wouldn't let him in. It's a nice area, poor Mum, the neighbours were scandalised and someone called the police. They took a while to come and by that time he'd flung a brick through Mum's front window. I don't know what he told the police but they calmed him down and he got in his car and left and they knocked on the door and spoke to us. They seemed to think we were living there so they thought it was just a domestic row but they did give me details of organisations and refuges but I had already googled that weeks ago. The truth is, even if you get a court order out against someone you can't stop them harassing you even if they get prosecuted for it later, which is actually unlikely unless they do you a serious injury and I'm not hanging around for that. He's sending me the most vile voice messages and threatening texts."

Sally finally stopped talking and Marie could think of nothing useful to say except that she was safe with them. Or so she hoped because presumably her own family were now targets.

"So where does he think you are now?" she asked.

"My brother is going over to stay with Mum for a couple of nights. She is really frightened and I'm so sorry I dragged her into it. What a mess. Anyway, I've told him to say I have gone to Scotland if Matthew comes back. I was at uni in Glasgow so it sounds likely but the truth is I don't know anyone there any more so it'll be a wild goose chase if he goes up north."

"Do you really think he would take it that far?" Marie asked.

"I know he's obsessive and he seems quite unhinged now so I wouldn't be surprised," Sally told her.

'No wonder she looks so dreadful and no wonder she found it so hard to leave,' Marie thought as she pulled into the farm yard and took Sally indoors. She showed her friend upstairs to their comfortable guest room.

"Oh, this is so lovely, I can't thank you enough," Sally sank down onto the edge of the bed; she had talked herself to a standstill and was now numb with fatigue.

"You sort yourself out and come down for some supper when you're ready," Marie told her gently and went downstairs to fill Henry in and reassure her children who had been told that Mummy had a friend who was in trouble and needed somewhere quiet to stay for a bit.

The family ate their bolognaise but Sally did not reappear and when Marie went up to check on her she found her curled up on the bed fast asleep. Marie's heart went out to her as she drew off her shoes and tucked a duvet round her as if she were one of the children.

'Let her sleep,' she thought, 'She's completely

exhausted.'

Sally slept late the following day but when she did appear she started to make herself useful tidying the kitchen.

"I can't tell you how grateful I am to you and Henry for taking me in," she said when Marie came in from feeding the chickens.

"I just need a bit of time to sort myself out and work out where I want to be."

"Yes, of course, you're still in shock," Marie told her, "you're welcome to stay as long as you need."

As it turned out, Sally was a perfect house guest; she had never had much to do with animals before but she fed the cats and Taffy, learned how much food the hens needed and shut them up in the evening. She soon took over much of the cooking and picked blackberries and the last of the apples to make pies for the freezer. She even helped Chloe with her homework.

Jack was the only member of the household who found her presence intrusive.

"It's not that I don't like her Mum," he confided, "But I want it to be just us, it feels all wrong when there's someone else here."

"It is different, darling, but Sally says she wants to stay in the area over the winter so she'll look for somewhere to rent. She's working at her translating you know so she's earning money."

In fact Sally was more than generous in paying for her keep, ordering a big shop online with some good wine and luxuries they didn't often buy. After supper she always went up to her room to work on her laptop, saying she had rather do it in the evenings and leave the days free for other things, but Marie suspected rightly that she was also conscious that the family welcomed some time on their own. She was starting to eat better and was losing the haggard look which George had noticed, saying to Henry,

"That young woman looks as if she's seen a ghost."

Henry told him she had just come out an abusive relationship.

"Ah, I know all about that," George replied, "Mavis had a cousin whose husband knocked her about something rotten. There was kiddies involved too, it was a bad business. Women couldn't get out of it in those days of course and no-one talked about it, not like they do now. Mavis used to hope she'd get her release one day but she died first and he lived to a ripe old age, the bugger. Odd thing was, he really seemed to grieve for her after. There's no accounting for folk."

Henry had to agree with him there.


When Henry went to the farm suppliers, Sally went with him, returning with a waxed jacket, some tough jeans and a pair of Hunter wellies so that she could go round the farm; she even cleaned out the chicken houses with Marie and walked up with Henry to check the sheep. She'd made rather a pet of Boris, taking him carrot and apple peelings, though the ponies nudged in to share those and now she asked when he would go in with the ewes.

"Not 'til mid-November," he told her, "but we've got to start feeding them now. The grass is going off, there's not so much nourishment in it and they need to be in prime condition when they conceive. That's going to be an expensive business though, it's roughly a kilo of sheep nuts for each ewe every day, divided into two feeds. We're setting up these long metal feeders, you see? You spread the food along so each ewe can get in to eat her share. "

"That's those big white bags in the stone building next to the calf sheds then?"

"That's right, 20 kg. bags so I won't be humping those around. I'll have to scoop it into smaller sacks and cart it up here. Of course Thomas and Josh have a quad bike, probably more than one in fact, but I can't justify that, at least not this year, and it's not worth getting the tractor out just to cart the feed around."

"I can see that," she said, "It's all hard work and time consuming though isn't it?"

"Yes, and all the feed has to be kept in that small stone building next to the calf sheds. I'm going to screw a steel plate to the back of the door right down to the ground to keep the rats out. I enjoy it though, it's very satisfying seeing the sheep looking so well. George is pleased with them anyway."

"He's great isn't he? He knows so much country lore of all sorts. I find it hard understanding his West Country accent sometimes though," she told him. "When will the lambs be born?"

" So,gestation is four and a half to five months, so if the ram goes in for a month, which is a cycle and a half, on November 1st., they should all be pregnant by the beginning of December which means lambing starts at the end of March. We could have gone earlier but since this is our first season we want to get the advantage of better weather. Mind you, if it's a wet spring we could be in trouble."

"How will you know if they're pregnant?" Sally asked.

"You can pay someone to come round and scan them, but I'm not sure if that's worth it with such a small flock, although that allows you to adjust the feed according to whether they are having single or twin lambs. The jury's out on that one. One thing we will do though is change the raddle every week and make a note of which ewes have been covered and when so we know when they are likely to lamb."

Henry was beginning to realise that their profits might be slimmer than he had hoped, given the price of feed, but the ewe lambs they bred would add to the flock and the males would be going to market at the end of next summer, which seemed a very long way off.

On Sunday morning, when Chloe was grooming the ponies with Tamsin and he found his mother busy preparing lunch with Sally, Jack decided to take Taffy out for a long walk.

He hadn't been out onto the moor for a while, so he set off up the hill with no clear direction in mind. The collie ran on ahead and he followed her lead until he rounded a gorse brake and again found himself near Lilian's caravan. This time her welcome was decidedly more cordial, in fact she seemed to be pleased to see him. She waved and he came over saying,

"I didn't mean to disturb you."

"Nonsense," she replied, "I was just putting the kettle on, do you want a mug of tea?"

For a moment Jack hesitated, wondering what foul

brew might come out of the caravan, but it seemed rude to refuse so he accepted and sat down on the steps. Lilian passed a tin mug out and a bowl with an encrusted spoon standing upright in a solidified lump of sugar. Jack sniffed at the tea, it smelt alright so he hacked a chunk off the sugar and stirred it in; it tasted fine.

"I'm making some breakfast scones, would you like some?"

Suddenly Jack was hungry and shortly Lilian emerged with a blackened frying pan containing golden fried balls of dough which broke into a light bread.

"They go well with bacon and egg of course but I don't have either at the moment, the hens are off lay, but you can have tomato sauce if you like, or they're good with jam."

Remembering the state of the sugar, Jack didn't want to risk the jam, and chose tomato ketchup, but to his surprise they were delicious on their own.

"How do you make them?" he asked indistinctly because his mouth was full.

"Just flour, self raising if you can get it, and milk. Drop the balls into hot fat and they just swell up. Turn them on all sides, that's it, done."

"Really? Just those two things? I'll tell Mum, they're great."

Lilian was pleased he liked them.

"How do you keep the milk though? Do you have a fridge?"

"No, it's long life milk, UHT."

Jack looked around at the empty hillside.

"It's a bit like camping isn't it?" he said. "How long have you lived in the caravan?"

She thought for a moment, "Must be fifteen years now just about."

"But you haven't always lived round here?"

"No, I came back here when I retired."

"Where were you before? If you don't mind me asking."

Lilian settled back with her chipped pottery mug of tea and looked into the distance. It wasn't often she had long conversations with people.

"I was a student at Cambridge, and then I lived in London for a while. That was where I met Anthony's father, he was in publishing but he owned the Hall at the time and I used to come down here for the long vacations."

"Were you friends with Anthony then? We've been to the Hall but we haven't met him yet."

"You'll meet him sometime I expect, but he's a bit of a recluse."

"What's a recluse?"

Lilian had forgotten that she was speaking to a child, but somehow that made it easier to talk.

"A recluse is someone who only wants to see people occasionally when it suits them. Anthony and I are about the same age but I didn't know him well in those days. He'd had a hard time at boarding school and then didn't really fit in at Oxford. He lived in Greece for several years and then in Goa, that was popular in the 1970's. All ancient history to you of course."

"I don't mind ancient history," said Jack. "Real ancient history I mean. We've done the Romans at school but I don't think very much of them. People think they were great with all their conquests and building roads and aqueducts and things but I don't think they were very civilised what with all the cruel games and crucifixions and stuff. I prefer the Greeks, they had proper heroes though their gods were much the same of course."

"You have read the Greek myths then?"

" I got a book out of the library at my old school, those stories are a lot cooler than modern superheroes. "

"I don't suppose you've read the Iliad have you?  The story of the Trojan war with Achilles and Odysseus?"

"Does the centaur come in that?"

"Chiron, yes".

" No,I haven't read it, but I've heard of him, and Jason and the golden fleece."

"I'll borrow a copy for you from the library at the Hall, I think you'll like it."

'What an unusual boy,' she thought.

"Won't they mind?" Jack had visions of her creeping in at dead of night and getting caught, he wouldn't put anything past this eccentric lady. She was fascinating though, none of his grand parents talked like this.

"No, I go down when I like and I often borrow books, Anthony won't mind. He just lives on the top floor now and the rest is divided up; not proper apartments  but people have sets of rooms, though there aren't many bathrooms and they have to share the kitchen. Still, I don't think most of them pay regular rent and they all seem to get on. I tried living there when I retired but it was too chaotic, too many people milling about,so I came up here."

Jack looked around at the caravan, thinking nothing could be more disorganised than the jumble of objects he could see inside. The shot gun was propped up ready to hand just inside the door, there was a bed or some sort of sofa piled high with blankets and a cat asleep on top, but the stove gave out a good heat and there was a hotplate for cooking, a rack of plates and mugs suspended on hooks. In fact the longer he looked the more he saw that there was a sense of order, not just a collection of random things crammed together as he had thought. Underneath the caravan was a pile of wood to keep dry and there was a shelter with a metal roof for the chickens. Inside the van he spotted a small let-down table with some sort of keyboard on it which caught his interest.

"Is that a laptop?" he asked.

"No," Lilian replied, "There's no electricity, so how would I charge it?"

"That's what I thought, so what is it?"

"It's a typewriter, an old Remington Rand, I've had it donkey's years. I use it to write articles for Somerset Life and the Exmoor Magazine and some academic journals too sometimes."

"Can I see?"

Lilian couldn't remember the last time she had let anyone over the threshold into the caravan, but she gestured for him to go in and look.

"You need ink ribbons and when you hit the keys it prints type."

"That's clever," he was impressed by its ingenuity.

"It's OK but you have to rub out your mistakes like in handwriting so you have to be careful how you type."

"Wow," said Jack,who was of course used to autocorrect and being able to delete.

"Right, you'd better be getting back, your mother will

be wondering where you are."

Suddenly Lilian felt she had revealed far too much of herself to this strange young man, yet she had enjoyed his visit.

"Sorry I asked so many questions," Jack sensed he was being dismissed. "I really would like to read that book, can I come back some time?"

"Yes alright," she conceded, "I'll go down to the Hall when I get round to it."

"Thank you Dr. Laidlaw," he was trying to be extra polite. "I won't tell my mother about the scones if you'd rather I didn't."

"Oh you can tell her if you like, maybe I'll come and meet her one day."

" I wish you would, she'd like that."

"Well, we'll see, off you go now."

Jack called for the dog and ran off down the hill jumping over clumps of stiff purple heather as Lilian stood at her caravan door, suddenly missing his bright company. She shook herself sternly,throwing off the unaccustomed sense of loneliness and headed for the stream to collect water.


Hannah and Sophie came over to look at the barn and see how many craft stalls it would hold. Sally joined the inspection and was able to offer some suggestions.

"It's a fantastic space," Hannah looked around at the long stone walls and high beamed roof, saying

" I reckon you could get eight or ten display stands in here and still have room for a few tea tables in the corner. If you had a counter and did tea and cake you'd make more profit and people would stay longer to browse."

"You could do cheese scones for a lunchtime alternative, even a ploughman's," Sally put in. "Anything quick to prepare on the spot, though there'd be a lot of baking to do while you're closed. It'd be a full-time job."

"Yes," Marie agreed, " It'd have to be worth while financially, but if it took off, maybe we could sell more eggs and when Henry has the poly tunnels up and running next year it would be a way to sell his produce direct to the public. If it was really successful we could even put in a mezzanine floor to accommodate more stands and maybe employ someone part-time. I'd like to set up my spinning wheel and loom in that corner where I could keep an eye on the whole area, I don't want to have a problem with shop lifting."

"No, and small items are easy to slip into a pocket," Sophie was thinking of her own rings and bracelets.

"Anyway, we're going to partition Henry's office off properly and sound proof it over the winter and I'll think about some decent flooring and how to arrange the lighting. I'd like to be open by Easter. I must say Sally, when you did that reading for me last spring I couldn't have imagined all these possibilities but I  see how accurate it was now."

"What kind of reading was this?" Hannah was intrigued."

"Oh, Sally is really good with the Tarot," Marie told her.

"Wow, would you be able to do one for me?" Hannah asked.

"And me," Sophie put in.

"Maybe I could come over to the Hall tomorrow," Sally suggested. She had the glimmer of an idea.

"That'd be great," Hannah agreed. "Could you come about 2.0 so we have time before school pick up?"

That arrangement made, they parted, Marie went to start supper while Sally offered to feed the hens and shut them up.

Going into the orchard, she bent to pick up a last large red apple which had fallen in good condition, and inadvertently brushed against a wasp which had landed on the fruit. The unexpected pain of the sting made her cry out, putting her hand to her mouth and suddenly she was overwhelmed with sorrow and self-pity, sinking down onto a projecting piece of stone wall, sobbing uncontrollably. For a few minutes the release of emotion was so strong she had no thoughts at all, just pouring out the grief and hopelessness of her situation, the culmination of so many months of stress.

She had been forced to control her feelings around Matthew for fear of provoking him, and when she left there was so much to do to extricate herself financially there had been no time to dwell on what she was losing. The sheer terror of his attack at her mother's home and her precipitate flight had to be brushed aside; she instinctively pulled herself together enough to be an acceptable house guest for the Freemans, but now the loneliness and insecurity of her position overwhelmed her. As the sobs subsided and she tried to dry her tears on the sleeve of her jacket she blamed herself.

'How could you let this happen? You always prided yourself on being clever and savvy but look at you now.

You're homeless, with no-one who really loves you, dependent on other people's charity.'

She now felt she couldn't trust herself to make any judgements, certainly where men were concerned and right now the thought of ever starting another relationship made her feel sick and weary.

'I can't go through all that again,' she thought, and that was a fresh source of grief because she had always wanted to find True Love. Now she felt that was an illusion, at least for her.

At last Sally got up and did the simple task she had come for, and the physical activity calmed her. The clucking fowl surrounded her as she filled their feeding bowls. The flock divided, hens flapping and squawking up the ramps into their respective houses to be shut up safely for the night.

'They all know what they're doing anyway,' Sally thought, 'They all  know where they belong. Seems they've got more sense than I have,' and that was a humbling thought.

As she walked back across the yard though, Sally's resilience emerged and she began to reason,

'You've got skills, you got yourself that translating job, that was an achievement given how down you were, and you can do that anywhere.'

She took a deep breath.

'OK, so now I have to find somewhere to live while I sort myself out. I can't put on the Freemans' good nature, kind as they are, for much longer. So that's the next thing to do.'

"I don't know what's happened to Sally, it's starting to get dark," Marie was concerned when  Henry came in.

"Oh, I saw her in the orchard a while ago, just having a quiet few minutes to herself I think," he replied.

A few moments later, Sally came through the door and Marie noticed her tear stained face but decided not to force a confidence.

"Supper's nearly ready," she told her.

"Be down in a minute, I'll just wash my hands."

Sally headed quickly for the stairs, but she soon reappeared and set the table as if nothing had happened. Whatever it was, the storm had passed, Marie surmised.

# Chapter 9

Sally was curious to see Mennad Hall; an odd name she thought, sounded vaguely Welsh, but then they were only a few miles from Wales across the Bristol Channel so maybe there was a connection. Walking through high wrought iron gates, now more rust than metal,Sally glimpsed the imposing frontage of the mansion and was struck by its eccentric design. It was asymmetrical with a rounded turret like a mediaeval keep at one end, with windows on all three levels. The rest of the Hall was an oblong, with three stories, each level marked by an intricate stone frieze of ivy leaves, while the drain pipes, where a mediaeval building might have gargoyles, sported panthers' heads out of which the roof water poured before being channelled down.

'How bizarre,' Sally was intrigued. 'It must mean something,' but the symbolism eluded her.

Her feet crunched loudly on the gravel and she rather hoped Hannah or Sophie might be looking out for her, but punctuality meant little to anyone at the Hall and the place seemed eerily deserted as she mounted the curved steps. The entrance was again guarded by stone panthers, each harnessed to a chariot. Sally hesitated before raising the heavy brass knocker in the same feline shape. The sound it made was thunderous and she stepped back, looking round again to examine the statues.

'Definitely not your standard lions,' she was thinking when she realised the door had been opened by a tall distinguished - looking older man, his grey hair pulled back in a pony tail, who was regarding her dispassionately.

For a moment neither of them spoke, and Sally had the odd impression that any explanation was superfluous, as if her presence was sufficient in itself. Nevertheless she obeyed convention and said that Hannah and Sophie had invited her.

"I was just admiring your statues. They don't look like conventional lions."

"They are panthers," he told her, standing back to let her enter the panelled hall where the ivy leaf motif ran riot over wainscotting and in wreaths of carved oak up the wide staircase. There was so much of it indeed that for a moment Sally felt quite claustrophobic as if the vines might close in and strangle her, but as she was struggling to take it all in, Hannah appeared, cheerful and open as ever, to greet her, saying,

"Anthony, this is our new friend Sally who is staying at the farm. Sally, this is Anthony Sinclair who owns the Hall."

Sally held her hand out and Anthony took it, making a half bow with old world courtesy, but evidently still with no interest in her personally. He turned and walked slowly up the stairs on thin stork like legs without looking back.

"Don't mind him," Hannah said as she led Sally towards the back of the house. "I don't know what he was doing down here anyway. He's just retreating to his eyrie."

Hannah took Sally into a large old-fashioned kitchen with a double- sized electric stove and a couple of tall

126

fridges.

"This is one of the communal rooms," she explained, looking first in one fridge and then in the other. "Oh, good, there is some milk," she confirmed. "Cup of tea?"

There were various mugs on the draining board and Hannah selected the cleanest and least chipped to offer Sally.

" I think we've got some herb teas if you'd rather?"

"Normal tea would be great, thank you." Sally was in no mood to be fussy.

Hannah left Sally briefly to call Sophie and by the time they returned, she had had a chance to sum up life in the shared house. 'Like house sharing at uni,' she thought.

They went through a side door out of the kitchen to Hannah's part of the house which she shared with her little daughter and her partner when he was around, which wasn't often as he was a roady with a band.

"This is the old servant's hall where they had their meals and socialised," she explained, leading the way through a large room which she obviously used as a work space. In the centre was a long deal table which had originally been in the kitchen, where she cut out the garments she made, with two sewing machines at the far end.

The next room, which had been the housekeeper's sitting room, was cosy, with a decorative fireplace , and then there were two smaller rooms which she used as bedrooms. Sally noticed a large set of brass bells still hanging in the servants' hall, each labelled so that servants could be summoned by wires to distant rooms which had lost their original use: drawing room, dining

127

room, morning room, billiard room, various bedrooms with odd names like Ariadne, Pentheus and Apollo; it must have taken an army of servants to run a house this big. She knew that after the first world war domestic staff was scarce and she wondered at what point decay had gradually set in.

Sally had brought her cards and did readings for both girls, Hannah first because of the school pick up, a land mark in the day which could not be allowed to slide. They were both delighted.

"You could make a living doing this," Sophie assured her, "Well, not down here maybe, but in Bristol or London."

Sally did not feel like going back to city life at the moment, and anyway, she had a more lucrative career if she wanted to do that. She accepted the compliment though and then asked,

" You all live in the house, then, how many of you are there?"

"So, ten people apart from Anthony. He has the whole of the top floor, but there are three couples and we have Phoebe of course, so you could say six separate groups," Hannah told her. "Most people have one or two rooms, there's plenty of space really. There are rooms that aren't even used in fact, and the library is still there, but hardly anyone goes in. There's just the one kitchen of course and not many bathrooms, but the electrics are alright and we all have kettles and microwaves and there are lots of fireplaces. No central heating of course, but there are loads of gas heaters if we buy cylinders. It's all very casual, no rules or anything, we get on."

"What's the arrangement for renting a room?" Sally

asked bluntly. She might as well be up front about it.

"For yourself you mean?" Sophie was surprised, Sally looked too well-heeled to end up in a place like this. Its faded elegance was somewhat over-rated when you were living in it.

"I would be interested yes. I'm staying with Marie at the moment as you know. I'm at a bit of a cross roads and I need somewhere for a while 'til I decide what I want to do next. I work online though, do you have internet?"

"Most of us just use our phones," Sophie told her.

"Anthony has a connection and you can pick it up in spots upstairs. He's funny about some things, very security conscious and careful of his privacy but I expect he'd give you the code if you lived here. Do you want me to go and ask him if he'll talk to you about moving in? I think it'd come better from one of us initially, Anthony doesn't do surprises."

"I'd be grateful if you would."

Hannah went to pick Phoebe up from school and Sally was left alone while Sophie went up to knock on Anthony's door.

'This could be a big mistake,' Sally thought, 'It's a real backward step after the flat, but it'd be temporary and I'd at least be out of the Freemans' hair. They've been great but they need their home back and I need some independence.'

After a while Sophie came back and said,

"Anthony would like to meet you in the library. I'll show you where it is; he doesn't let anyone into his private apartments if he can help it."

Sophie took Sally upstairs and along a corridor where

a door at the further end opened into one of the rooms in the turret. She turned back at the door, leaving Sally to enter the room on her own, finding herself literally surrounded by books. The circular space, punctuated by three long windows, was filled floor to ceiling by volumes,many leather bound and the most modern appearing to date to the 1970's. The room was furnished with two fine mahogany tables set with matching chairs.

By one window, which commanded what must once have been a fine view of the formal gardens, were two leather armchairs, stuffed with horsehair and still surprisingly comfortable. Sally was suddenly excited by the prospect of exploring the room. Judging by the dust, there were no regular visitors. She turned to face the door as Anthony entered, feeling guilty as if she had been caught taking too great an interest, but he motioned her to a seat by the window, saying,

"I see you are a lover of books."

"I have to confess that I am." No point in denying it.

"I'm afraid I am rather a philistine in that respect, any interest I had was drummed out of me at school, and later at Oxford. It's no use, you know, if a child is forced to learn by rote what does not interest him. He quickly comes to hate the whole business of education."

"I can see that would be true."

Sally wasn't humouring him; she had little experience with children but put like that she could imagine the small boy with his nose stuck in a Latin primer having to pursue uncongenial studies year on year because it was expected of him. Doubtless he didn't shine either which must have made it so much worse.

Sensing her sympathetic spirit, Anthony said,

"So you think you might like to stay with us at the Hall?"

She was surprised at her own sincerity, saying,

"I think I would like that very much. I believe it may be exactly what I need."

"Serendipity then." He nodded. "Sophie said you need to use the internet, what is it you do?"

"I do technical translations from German to English, Chemistry research papers mainly."

"Do you?"

She couldn't tell if that meant anything to him.

"I'm a research chemist myself you see," she explained,"And I grew up in Switzerland."

"Nothing to do with blogs and social media or anything like that? No newspaper reporting?"
"Absolutely not," she assured him, "Dry  scientific research. A very limited number of academics are interested in the results. "

"Well I have no objection to that," he said decisively. "I will give you my Wi-Fi code and you can work in here, the router is in the room above you see."

"Ah, that is very kind of you."

He nodded his head in acquiescence.

"You may tell Sophie we are in agreement."

He gave her another half bow as he turned to the door.

"She will tell you of the arrangements."

He left her feeling strangely elated, she didn't know why, given the state of the shared accommodation, but somehow virtually sole use of the library made up for a lot.

Sophie reappeared as if by magic and led her one

flight down to the equivalent turret room on the ground floor. What its original purpose might have been Sophie couldn't tell, maybe just a boot room or the flower room, for it had French doors to the garden, but it was now furnished with a four poster bed complete with peacock blue silk hangings, a massive mahogany wardrobe and matching dresser and a brocade chaise longue which looked as if it belonged in an Oscar Wilde play.

"Anthony suggested you might like this room. Sorry about the furniture, Zak and Polly dumped it in here when they took a room upstairs. I actually think theirs was Anthony's mother's room before she ran off to Florence with an Italian count."

'Poor Anthony,' Sally thought, 'He hasn't had much luck has he?'

"It's fine," she said, "I really like it. What's the rent by the way?"

"Is thirty five pounds a week OK?" Sophie was tentative, it sounded like a lot to her. She only paid twenty five and that was when she could afford it. There's a bathroom on the half landing, the shower's electric so it makes its own hot water but the flow's not great."

'Whatever,' thought Sally ; she'd had enough sensory impressions for one day, good and bad, so she took Sophie's word for it.

When Sally told Marie of her decision to take a room at the Hall, there were mixed emotions in the family. Jack was delighted, he had been spending increasing amounts of time outdoors or in his room. Marie was relieved in a way but she felt guilty that Sally felt she should go.

"Are you sure?" she asked, "You know we enjoy having you, and it's all a bit basic round there."

"I've got to make a start at getting my life together, and it's only a half way house. If I decide to spend the winter on Exmoor I'll look for a cottage to rent; it's not as if I can't afford to do that. Meanwhile I'll be saving money, it's ridiculously cheap, and it's a really interesting house. You should see the library!"

Marie said she had seen it, and agreed it was fascinating.

"Well, I'll lend you some bedding and towels and come over with you to clean your room at least."

" That's really kind. When I think of all the good stuff I left at the flat I feel sick, but hey, it's all replaceable I guess. If you've got time to help, that would be great. You've all been wonderful, but it's time I stood on my own two feet."

Henry was pleased when he heard the news; he liked Sally and she was an easy guest to have around, but he preferred to have the place to themselves.

"After all, she'll only be up the lane," he told Marie, "You can see her as often as you like."

'I must stop feeling responsible for her,' Marie thought. 'She's a capable person,she can make her own decisions, but she still needs support.'

The following day, they took a mop and bucket and a vacuum cleaner round to thoroughly clean Sally's room. The floor was tiled in black and white, a legacy of its utilitarian past.

"It's cold on your feet," Marie complained.

"There may be a solution to that, let's have a scout around," Sally suggested.

They found a storeroom full of bits and pieces, including two faded Persian rugs and a long pair of dark blue velvet curtains to cover the outside door, which instantly gave the room a feeling of warmth.

"We're just relocating them in the house, I get the impression everyone makes use of whatever they can find," Sally said.

Marie had brought a mattress topper, rightly suspecting the mattress would be questionable, but after they had vacuumed the bed and made it up, the room looked surprisingly comfortable.

"I really like it," Sally said, glancing around her circular apartment. "I'm going to appropriate a couple of those gas heaters we saw, and put one in the library and one in here."

Marie put the empty cylinders in the Volvo's capacious boot and promised to swap them for full ones when she went into town.

So Sally became one of the Communards, as Henry called them,

"Though they're hardly likely to man the barricades," he joked, "They're so laid back they're practically horizontal."

At first Sally felt as if she was on some sort of New Age retreat, everything was so unfamiliar that she fell into a kind of Zen mindfulness state, letting it all wash over her from one minute to the next; this new existence seemed surreal.

She used the library for her work. Anthony had left an envelope on one of the   tables addressed to her, Miss Sally Grainger, in flowing black script. Finding it contained the internet code, she thought,

'He's really not as out of it as he seems, he must have got my surname from the standing order I set up.'
She was soon on casual friendly terms with the other residents and sometimes joined them for a coffee in the kitchen, where there was often a group chatting round mealtimes. Sometimes there would be a big shared stir fry or bolognaise if anyone felt like making it, and word would spread round the house so that people congregated.

Sally got into the habit of cooking for everyone from time to time and in that way she quickly became part of the extended family, who all looked out for each other. Otherwise however, she didn't bother to prepare food for herself and lived mostly on Ryvita, cream cheese, yoghurt and the occasional chocolate bar. The stove was never clean, the sink was always full of dishes, and having opened the two oven doors once, she couldn't bring herself to brave that again. She didn't lose the weight she had gained staying at the farm but she wasn't putting any on and she still had an air of fragility about her.

The library became her refuge and her solace, and as the days got chilly, when she was not working she curled up in one of the leather chairs in front of the rusty square gas heater she had dragged up there and immersed herself in the books. In this way, Sally became familiar with the layout of the shelves, finding a system of sorts with sections on history or travel and she was surprised to find Goethe's poetry and plays among the literature.

It was some time before she thought to open a set of cupboards and discovered a pile of old photograph albums which she found so intriguing she set herself to identify the people and settings, and piece together the Sinclair family history.

Sally put the albums in order, judging by the clothing of people in the photos. The early ones were black and white, mainly featuring Gerard Sinclair whom she identified by one shot of him posed by his easel, brush in hand and incongruously dressed in a formal Edwardian suit with a flowing cravat.

'You wouldn't want to get paint on those clothes,' she thought, this was evidently the equivalent of a publicity shot. He was certainly handsome, with an enigmatic gaze, which he probably cultivated, she thought. Other pictures were more informal, Gerard always front and centre in any group, whether it was on the terrace of a grand hotel in Nice, promenading along the Croisette at Cannes or carefully posed with friends on the lawns in front of the Hall.

The next album was less formal; taken exclusively at the Hall it seemed, with some early hand tinted colour pictures. The scenes mainly featured young women wearing diaphanous gowns and circlets of flowers cavorting together in the grounds, chasing one another through shrubbery, leaning against tree trunks or posed in classical groups as if caught frozen in action, which reminded Sally of scenes from Greek vases she had seen in the British Museum.

So, these must be members of the cult which Marie had mentioned. It all looked rather theatrical and innocent; Sally had heard about Isadora Duncan and the early twentieth century enthusiasm for healthy living through exercise in nature, which grew into nudity, naturism and the Health Through Joy movement.

'I suppose that was all a back lash against tight corsets and all those social conventions restricting women. The suffragettes certainly had their work cut out.'

Sally was only too aware that there was still a fair way to go in the struggle for equality.

'I bet those women were all under Gerard's spell, we really don't help ourselves do we?'she thought bitterly.

The next album of colour photos seemed to date from the 1950's and 60's, and was much more conventional. In the first pages an attractive couple were photographed against the back drop of the Hall. The man bore a striking resemblance to Gerard, so presumably these would be Anthony's parents. His mother was slim and stylish in a dress with nipped in waist and full skirt, long fingers elegantly curved around a cigarette holder.

Other shots were taken inside the hall, giving an insight into how it would have been during its heyday, when, judging by the pictures, house parties with dinners and dancing were regular events. The men wore dinner suits, the women evening dresses and she recognised some of the rooms, especially the dining room which was still distinctive because there was a leather frieze around the walls depicting some sort of hunting scene.

There seemed to be a gap in time and then the second half of the album contained pictures which she judged to date from the 1960's. The formal dinners seemed to be a thing of the past, now Gerard's son appeared informally with various friends, many of them younger because he now looked as if he was in his late forties. These were casual unposed snaps taken, it seemed, by various people, some in Polaroid which had faded.

One striking young woman appeared frequently, with an elfin crop of dark hair and an interesting piquant face, not beautiful but she somehow drew the eye.

The sophisticated wife no longer featured, and now this young woman seemed to be intimate with the owner of the Hall, bending over his shoulder, seated on the grass, leaning against his chair smiling at the camera, or laughing up into his face.

One notable aspect of all these pictures through the decades was that no children appeared. There was no sense of family life through the generations, the record was entirely social as if that aspect of life was all that mattered. Flicking back through the albums, Sally looked more closely at that leather frieze and suddenly she wanted to see it for herself.

Hannah told her that Judith, who had a pottery workshop, occupied the dining room, so that evening she asked her about the hunting scene.

"Come and have a look if you like, it's certainly interesting; in fact when I first moved into the room I found it a bit disturbing but now I'm used to it, it's blended into the furniture if you know what I mean."

When she came to examine it, Sally thought it would take a lot for her to live with that imagery, once you knew what it was. The dark embossed leather strip, about a hundred centimetres deep, encircled the room at shoulder height. It was not a conventional hunting scene however, with hounds and horses and huntsmen, but the quarry which appeared at intervals, seemed to be young men, looking fearfully over their shoulders, pursued by wild women on foot, each brandishing a spear or some other weapon. There was the usual trailing ivy which featured everywhere in the Hall, entwining in such a way that it obscured some of the action and you had to look intently to work out what was actually going on. Some of the women seemed to be accompanied by panthers, although these might have been hunting on their own account because deer also appeared among the foliage so that it was unclear whether the young men had turned into deer or vice versa.

Obviously this odd scene had been part of the original decoration of the Hall; was it possible that the guests in their evening dress had failed to notice their surroundings? Well it was just obscure enough that they probably didn't, Sally thought. She found it very unsettling.

One day she was sitting as usual in the library, working on a translation, when the door opened and a stranger walked into the room. Sally was surprised, no-one else ever used the library, but this woman acted as if she had every right to be there.

"Good Morning," she said, and made straight for the literature section across the room. Sally could not help speculating about her; she looked like a tramp, but there was something genteel in her bearing and speech completely at odds with the faded brown mackintosh with its belt which seemed to be made of braided baler twine. Of all things,she was wearing gum boots. Sally was amused to note that she was now able to identify baler twine in all its rural uses; she'd learned a lot in the last few weeks. She was smiling at this thought when the visitor turned round, and surveyed her in turn.

Lilian, whose years as a lecturer had honed her observation, recognised a fellow intellectual when she saw one, but noted her underlying air of vulnerability.

"Could you pass me the steps from behind your chair?" she asked. "I believe the volume I'm seeking is on the top shelf'."

Sally leapt to her aid; no-one her age should be teetering on the library steps stretching for something virtually out of reach.

"Let me fetch it," she offered, carrying the heavy steps across the room. "What are we looking for?"

"Pope's Homer's Iliad," was the reply. "It's a brown squarish edition, I think I see it up there."

"Ah yes," said Sally, who found she was herself not too happy up this ladder. "Do you want the Odyssey too?"

"Not at the moment, I don't think, see how we get on with the Iliad first."

Sally descended and handed her the book.

"Are you doing some particular research?" she asked, wanting to continue engaging this strange woman in conversation; it would be irritating if she just disappeared without any explanation, and anyway, this translation was tedious and she needed a break.

"Oh no, this is for Jack, a young friend of mine."

"Jack Freeman? From Holtbourne?" Sally didn't know why she even asked, it seemed so unlikely, but he was the only Jack she knew.

"That's right, do you know him?"

"I was staying at the farm with the family," Sally told her, "But I wouldn't say I know Jack very well."

'Or at all it seems,' she thought, discomforted at having  dismissed Jack as a typical surly boy who resented her intrusion. She certainly wouldn't put him down as a Greek scholar in the making.

"He's an unusually perceptive boy," Lilian told her, " with an interest in the ancient world."

Sally began to think this rather dotty old woman had taken a shine to Jack for some reason and that she was due to be disappointed if she offered him an eighteenth century translation of an ancient Greek text by an individual who may or may not have existed. He'd probably rather meet the heroes via a blockbuster or a video game. She was recalled by Lilian asking,

"So you are the scientist Anthony mentioned, you're doing some translations?"

"That's right."

'Hmmm...she's on visiting terms with Anthony then, more than can be said for the rest of us.' Sally was curious.

She sat down in one of the leather chairs and Lilian took the hint and joined her.

"You're a friend of Mr. Sinclair I take it?"

"My connections with the family go way back," Lilian confirmed.

Sally seized her chance.

"I hope you don't mind my asking but what do you know of the history of the Hall? I know Gerard Sinclair was an artist who built it, what, during the Edwardian period. I've seen some of his pictures, they're a bit Pre-Raphaelite meets Art Nouveau if that isn't too disrespectful, a lot of nymphs and shepherds and some quite striking landscape. But what about the cult, someone mentioned  Dionysius or Bacchus?"

"My dear girl," Lilian rose to the bait. "There's a world of difference  between Dionysius and Bacchus. The Roman god Bacchus was a crude copy, a gross pastiche riding about on an ass with his drunken followers, while Dionysius is a much subtler figure. His cult originated in India and spread to Greece. His symbols are the ivy you see carved everywhere at the Hall, the fennel which you find growing wild in the grounds and of course his chariot was drawn by panthers. In essence he has been known in many cultures and by other names. His Celtic equivalent is Cernunnos, the Lord of the Wilds, the horned nature god who rules animal fertility and gathers the beasts in harmony.

Of  course, human society does not promote harmony so the dark side prevails. In the Greek world women, apart from priestesses and a few notable intellectuals, were  chattels useful only for breeding, so naturally any cult offering emotional release in an acceptable ritual form took hold. Have you heard of the Maenads, from the Greek for madness? "

"Didn't they dance into an ecstatic frenzy? Oh, yes, and didn't they tear young men apart in their rituals. Is that's what's going on in the library?"

"Exactly so."

"But surely Gerard Sinclair's young women didn't go that far? "

"Well, no, there was a scandalous incident when a young man was injured in the woods and it was a brief sensation even in the London papers, but Exmoor was still a remote area and the details were unclear. He was probably attacked by a wild beast, that may of course be the origin of the legend of the Beast of Exmoor, and though in recent years many people claim to have seen big cats, maybe it's not a recent phenomenon."

"Do you mean Gerard actually kept panthers?"

"I really don't know, but I have wondered. By the time I knew the Hall, the cult had ceased to exist; none of them were local of course, soon after the scandal they drifted back to Bloomsbury or wherever they came from and it all went quiet.

Gerard's son Edwin was in publishing and spent most of his time in London. Many of the smaller publishing houses were taken over or amalgamated in the 1970's, it was hard for the smaller businesses to keep going in a more international market, and eventually Edwin retired down here. Anthony is the last of the Sinclairs and as you see, the glory days are over."

Sally was still thinking about the mystery cult.

"There's a scene in Thomas Mann's novel The Magic Mountain where the protagonist goes up the Zauberberg and has a vision of the three ages of women, the Virgin, the Witch and the Crone. When he gets close he realises they are carving up a baby; the fear of women's power goes very deep doesn't it?"

"Oh, the persecution of witches through the ages is testimony to that," Lilian agreed.

It suddenly occurred to Sally to ask,

"But why did Gerard choose this particular spot to build the Hall? Was it just that Exmoor was so remote in those days?"

"Oh hardly, it was very popular with the hunting set in his day and there are many country houses which were built as hunting boxes. That may be how he first came here, I suppose. No, he wasn't a complete charlatan you know, he believed in his rites, they were a form of nature worship. He claimed there was a portal here, that is why he chose the farm, because of course that was here for centuries before he built the Hall."

"What kind of a portal? Do you mean a gateway into the Underworld, like at Delphi?"

"No, I believe it was the other way round, some power released from a gateway or portal in the landscape. Well, you aren't getting much work done are you? Thank you for getting the book down for me."

She rose a little stiffly to leave and then, turning back, and offering a hand to shake,

"I am Lilian Laidlaw by the way."

"Sally Grainger."

As they shook hands, Sally looked closely at the older woman's face for the first time and a realisation dawned. Beneath the lines of age she glimpsed the face of the charismatic young woman so often photographed at the Hall with Edwin Sinclair.

When Sally described her meeting in the library to Marie, she was more interested in Lilian Laidlaw than the history of the mystery cult.

"So, it's true, Anthony's father was her lover? And that's what gives her the right to live on the estate? And she really was a university lecturer? You wouldn't think it to look at her now would you?"

Marie had caught a glimpse of Lilian at a distance in the village.

"Oh yes, I found a copy of the local history book she wrote in the library. It's mainly myths and legends really, like the story of Dead Woman's ditch, the neolithic forts like Bury Castle and the leper colony that was supposed to exist at Culbone. It's well-written though. I think it's still in print, you could get a copy from the Tourist Information Centre. Holtbourne gets a mention because of the spring which is supposed to have healing properties as you know."

Sally realised however that Marie wasn't interested enough to buy the book.

# Chapter 10

There was enough to keep Marie occupied on the farm. The first frosts of autumn left rime on the grass in the morning and keeping the house warm became a priority. They decided to invest in a wood burner for the sitting room fireplace which entailed paying for a costly liner to protect the chimney.

"It doesn't exactly go with the marble fireplace," Henry observed ruefully, "But it stops most of the heat going up the chimney and we can open the doors if we want to see the open fire."

The children picked up fallen chestnuts at the edge of the wood to roast on top of the wood burner, although you had to be careful they didn't burst and fly across the room. They had to pay for a large load of seasoned logs which was expensive but Henry took Jack up into the woods with the chainsaw to cut up a trailer full of fallen branches to dry out for later. As they climbed onto the tractor to take the load down to the farm they heard a loud groaning bellow echoing down off the moor behind.

"The rut has begun and a stag must have taken his stand up there," said Henry. "We can go up and look, when we've unloaded this lot."

Jack was elated, he couldn't wait to go and see this raw natural spectacle unfolding. It was late afternoon when the family walked up the track and a mist was coming in. They located the great red deer stag standing in an open arena on the top of the moor, his head raised, heavy antlers thrown back, issuing his challenge which echoed around the hillside. The deep hoarse sound was disturbing even when you knew what it was.

"It's so elemental " Marie said, as she hugged Chloe to her side. Chloe had her hands over her ears.

"It's too loud," she complained.

Already a group of hinds had joined the stag who was in his prime, powerful and proud. As they watched, a younger stag appeared in the distance but did not approach.

"We've left it a bit late, it'll be dark soon, but now he's chosen his spot he'll hold this territory for a couple of weeks at least so we'll have plenty of chance to come up again," Henry told them.

"We must get some good photos too," said Marie.

Jack was keen to ask George what he knew about the stag's behaviour and as usual George was happy to share his knowledge.

"Deer have their habits you see," he explained. "You know about the racks they use, you can't put them off using those trails. If you build a fence across one they will jump it or knock it down, that's how a lot of deer get injured or they keep getting run over at the same place on a road.

All grazing animals are like that of course, they find what they think is a safe path and use it all the time. That's why you see sheep paths through the heather and even those two ponies follow the same paths across the field and you won't see them both lying down at once, one is always standing guard in case there's a predator. Now the rut is the same, those stands at different places on the moor are used year after year for generations and you'll always hear stags bolving there.

The prime stags gather all the hinds and herd them up so no-one else can get a look in, that makes sure the fittest breed you see. The odd hind or two will be stolen away by a young stag now and then but the big boys are prepared to fight it out, so you will hear two stags bellowing, answering each other. That deep sound travels a long distance."

"I know, you can hear it at the farm for hours sometimes. But do they really fight and injure each other?"

"Well that's a last resort if they're very evenly matched," George told him. "Usually it's a stand off and one backs down, maybe after the biggest stag runs at the other one. That's what the antlers are for. If he has Brow, Bay and Trey, a full rack of antlers, he's in his prime and until he gets too old he'll be at the top for several years. Eventually a young mature stag will take over, but that lets a different blood line in, it's nature's way."

"What happens to the old stags then?" Jack was feeling sorry for them.

"If he's not badly injured he may still attract a small harem and keep out of the way of the main rut. There are no predators now like wolves to kill off an old animal and outside the rutting season you will see groups of two or three bachelor stags hanging out together so they don't do too badly."

In the following weeks the stags bolved night and day. Chloe got used to it and Henry and Marie often found it amusing, but for Jack it had a visceral effect and he became even more attuned to the power in the landscape and the music it produced.

Now the high tinkling notes of summer gave way to a more strident and insistent rhythm, though still so faint that he often sensed rather than actually heard it. At night, wrapped in his duvet against the cold, he opened his window and gazed at its source on the Tump where again he discerned a figure seated on the summit. The notes now were deeper and sometimes Jack heard the long drawn out call of a horn, not the rallying cry of the hunt but a compelling summons.

Towards the end of October, Marie messaged Sally to come for coffee since she hadn't seen her for a while.

" How are things going with you then?" Sally asked.

"It's all fine really."

From Marie's tone, Sally was unconvinced.

"OK, out with it,come on, what's wrong?"

"Nothing, I'm just a bit fed up. Henry and I never get to go out together as a couple and I suppose I've realised that's how it is now. We always had Mum to fall back on for babysitting before. Ellie asked if we wanted to go for a meal at the pub, it's the acoustic night on Saturday, not the Folk night but an open Mic evening with various performers. They've got Thomas's mum coming for the night. I nearly asked if our two could do a sleep over but it's a bit of a cheek and anyway, Chloe wouldn't want to go if it's all boys."

"So what's the problem? I can look after your kids, they know me well enough by now."

Marie hadn't thought of Sally as childcare material.

"Are you sure?"

"Well it's not as if there are nappies to change, they're good kids and they're too young to organise a rave in your absence. We can hunker down and watch E.T or something and make a movie night of it with pop-corn. "

"Are you sure you don't mind?"

"I'm definitely up for it, it'll be fun and it's not as if I have anything more scintillating to do with my evenings."

Marie hugged her, "Sally, you're a star!"

When Henry heard the news, he was pleased for Marie's sake although privately he wasn't over enthusiastic about the local music element to the evening. Still, it was a chance for them to get out and maybe if it went well they could do something classier next time, like a romantic dinner at the Gastro pub instead of The Plough.

"It's this weekend then," Sally confirmed.

"Yes, I've got to go up to the office next week," Henry told her.

"Oh really? I hope you don't mind me asking, but would it be much out of your way to drop me off at the station on your way to the motorway?"

"No, I can go that way, you're welcome."

"Where are you going?" Marie was surprised.

"I'd like to visit my mother. We've been talking on What's App but I haven't seen her since, well, you know, I left in such a hurry. I want to be sure she's alright and also, it sounds funny, but I've been thinking about her life and I want to find out if she's happy. I've been so wrapped up in my own self-centred bubble for a couple of years and I've neglected her. I feel bad about it."

"She's OK though, isn't she?" Marie asked.

"She has her book club and aquarobics, she goes on holiday with a friend, but those things don't necessarily add up to a satisfying life do they? She doesn't have a partner or anything. My brother's better at seeing her than I am and I feel sad about that."

"Well, let me know when you want to come back and I'll meet your train," Marie offered.

"I think I'll stay a week and come back the following Monday, but maybe I can find some way of getting back without troubling you. I wish I'd learned to drive, but living in the city it never bothered  me before."

Ellie was pleased that Marie had found a sitter. They were looking at the menus when she asked, "And this is the friend you told me about? The one who had the abusive partner."

"Sally, that's right. I don't think you've met her."

"Is she tall, with long wavy hair? I wondered who that was, I've noticed her in the village. You should introduce us."

"I will, she only knows the people at the hall."

"Is she staying at that dump?"

'Why does Ellie have to be so judgemental?' Marie wondered, irritated by her manner.

"It's only temporary," she replied, "She's away next week but I'm collecting her from the train next Monday, so come for coffee after that and you can meet her."

"I can pick her up if you like," Ellie suggested. "I have to take the boys into Taunton at half term for new school shoes, I might as well do it on that Monday if it saves you the trouble."

Marie agreed; she was glad not to have to waste a couple of hours going to the station, but she felt guilty at exposing  Sally to a possible  barrage of insensitive questions. Come to think of it though, Sally could deflect unwelcome enquiries better than anyone she knew.

On Monday as they drove to the station, Henry was getting into city mode.

"It's a different way of thinking," he told Sally,"everything goes up a gear."

"I know exactly what you mean,"she said. "Working from home, you get the job done but there isn't that buzz, you only communicate when it's necessary."

"Yes, exactly, and I sense I'm missing the finer nuances, what's going on under the surface in the office. It's not as if no-one else is working from home some of the time, but they can go in if something needs discussing and they're all still office based."

Those next few days he found he had a lot to catch up on; the company was hoping to gain two new clients. Henry thought he had not quite been kept in the loop. At a distance he hadn't picked up on the importance of one of them and everyone was on tenterhooks at work to see whether they would be awarded the contract. After a couple of days in the office however, he felt he was up to speed and was becoming excited by the prospect of his own involvement. That gave him something to talk to his father about and they managed to have an amicable discussion.

"One new client is virtually in the bag, it's pretty standard stuff, a family firm that wants to sell out to a bigger company so they want to position themselves in the marketplace. The other one is really important, it'll be a coup if we land the contract. It's a major company planning complete restructuring, ditching some product lines, developing new technology, a complete modernisation to stay competitive. They're a household name so it would be great for us if we get it."

"I'm glad to see you showing some enthusiasm," his father told him. "I was afraid that you were losing your edge and ditching your career for a lifestyle you really can't afford for at least another twenty years."

"I know I need to keep working Dad, it's a balancing act, but now the house is liveable and there's less to do on the farm in the winter, this has come at the right time for me."

"I certainly hope so. You can't afford to lose your drive now, there are plenty of young men who would like to be in your shoes."

"I'm aware of that, Dad."

As usual Henry was left feeling he could never do enough to prove himself to his father.


As it happened, Marie's fears were unfounded; Ellie and Sally seemed to get on  fine, so well in fact that Ellie offered her one of their holiday cottages as a winter let from  mid-November and Sally was delighted to accept. Marie wondered if the prospect of some extra income was behind Ellie's offer of a lift in the first place, but if so, it suited both of them.

On the first of November George arrived early to supervise Basil's introduction to his harem.

"You've got him in fine condition," he commented, surveying the ram with a critical eye. "He's not a bad tup you know. The Exmoor Horn should be short coupled, strong stocky legs, flat back, and he's all of that. He should throw some good lambs for you. Let's introduce him to the ladies, but first we need to put the harness on him. You've been handling him quite a bit haven't you, so that shouldn't be too difficult. Let's have a bucket of feed and see if you can get it on him."

Henry slotted the bar of oily bright green raddle into the box on the breast of the harness and approached Basil with some misgivings. With his head in a feed bucket however Basil was quite amenable, he'd been here before many times. Henry shook the bucket while the whole family looked on, and led Basil out of the ponies' paddock and up the track to the top fields where the ewes raised their heads, aware that something new was happening.

When Henry let Basil into the field he immediately approached the ewes, neck outstretched, scenting any that were in season. He followed first one and then another, most walking away from him and rejecting his advances since they were not yet ready to mate. Within five minutes though, one ewe had stood for him, switching her tail and he mounted her, so briefly that Henry and Marie doubted the mating could have been successful, but George laughed, saying,

"Oh they don't mess about, they just get on with it. He knows what he's about anyway, you can leave him to it."

The tell- tale smudge of green on the ewe's back marked her out and as that faded Marie would brighten the streak again so that she could identify those which would lamb early. The following week they changed the raddle to red and so on until all the ewes had been covered as they came into season.

The clocks had changed; as the days grew shorter and

the nights were cold, sounds carried in the stillness. Owls hooted in the dark, each species with a different call; the barn owls with their familiar screeches and hissing noises, which the family had heard all summer as the parents flew back and forth at dusk to feed their chicks, but there were other piping sounds they found harder to identify. They heard the eerie scream of the vixen and the bark of the dog fox echoing around the farm in the frosty night air.

The badgers had retreated to their set where the sow would give birth to her cubs and lie in until spring, squirrels still scurried through the branches on sunny days but the rabbits ventured out of their burrows less often and were now seldom spotted. After the rut, deer still hung around the hill,coming down into the higher fields for better grass and sheltering in the wood away from the wind and lashing rain.

Sally wrote a polite note to Anthony, telling him that she had rented a cottage locally and thanking him for letting her stay at the Hall when she was in need of accommodation. She 'appreciated his kindness'. She received a courteous reply, so she felt her stay was ending amicably. In the last two weeks she became more friendly with Judith, the potter, and spent time in her studio, dabbling in clay again. She was able to help correct a glaze which was not firing well; a knowledge of chemistry had many uses. Sally was beginning to feel more like her old self, rediscovering interests  from the time before she met Matthew, and she was pleased when Judith suggested she could make use of the workshop sometimes.

"There's usually some space in the kiln for the odd extra pot when I'm firing," she said.

On the last evening Sally even felt a little sad to be leaving the Hall, it had a unique atmosphere she was going to miss. She visited the library for the last time and thought fondly of the hours she had spent there, it had been a healing and calming space for her. Her quirky bedroom with its massive furniture held a charm too, but she was definitely not going to miss the shabby bathroom and chaotic kitchen arrangements, nor the winter chill which was inexorably creeping into the fabric of the old building.

# Chapter 11

Marie picked Sally up, cramming her various belongings into the back of the Volvo and set out for
Handy Cross on the other side of the village.

"I'm sure the cottage will have all mod cons, you have to provide everything these days with holiday lets, but the downside is you'll be further out of the village."

"I don't mind that, I can walk in to the village and I'll get a food order delivered. It'll be such a luxury to have a fridge of my own. It's funny how I am appreciating the small things I used to take for granted."

Sally had not been to the farm before and looked around with interest as Marie pulled up in front of the cottage. A wide entrance had brought them into the square which had once been the old farmyard; the new set of agricultural  buildings were now set to the rear of the complex. The farmhouse, set to one side behind a walled strip of front garden sat opposite  two holiday cottages which each had a small patio garden overlooking the fields behind. Across the large courtyard was a big stone barn which was obviously being converted to a house; the windows were in place and it seemed to be nearing completion.

"Here we are then, Ellie said it's the first cottage."

Marie tried the door but it was locked. She was about to knock at the farmhouse when Josh appeared. He waved, calling,

"Hi Marie, I've got the key. Ellie's had to go out."

Watching his tall slim figure stride towards them Sally thought,

"This is the brother then, he's not what I expected at all."

He came up and for a moment their eyes met in unguarded appraisal before each glanced away in some confusion. She was struck by his cool grey gaze and air of self possession, he was surprised by her beauty and unconscious elegance, she was far from Ellie's description of a downtrodden, abused little woman. The door was opened and they went inside; the old farm labourer's cottage was small but had been completely modernised. With comfortable furnishings and neutral décor it made up in cleanliness and convenience for any lack of character. Sally thought it was just what she wanted and Josh's heart skipped a beat as he caught her warm smile.

'She's bloody gorgeous,' he thought, followed by 'steady now,' habitually putting the brakes on.

"Oh this is great," she said with open delight, "Thank you, this is just what I need."

Josh pulled himself together to show them the practical aspects of living in the cottage.

"There's a welcome book with instructions for the heating and washing machine and so on. The WiFi code is here on the router."

Marie went out to open the boot and there was a moment when Josh and Sally's hands brushed reaching for the same suitcase.

"Let me help you with that," he said, recovering the situation.

He left them to it soon afterwards and Marie, who

had been too busy unpacking to notice the frisson in the air, kept asking how Sally wanted the kitchen cupboards arranged and what to put where.

It wasn't until she had also left that Sally was able to close the front door which led straight into the sitting room and sank onto the sofa to take stock. With the prospect of her own home in normal surroundings, Sally felt in one sense more herself than she had in a long time. But with returning self confidence she was also aware of an unwelcome and unexpected reawakening of interest in men, or to be more accurate, one man in particular.

Her sudden attraction to Josh was disconcerting and she didn't know whether to be pleased or not that it seemed to be mutual. That caused a panicky feeling; 'don't let this get out of control, you're not ready to get into all that again, and anyway, all he's done is show an interest. With those looks he's probably a player, you'd better watch yourself.'

She couldn't know that Josh was also disconcerted by the encounter. These days he was guarded in his reactions to women and he was afraid to fan this flame which had sprung up in an instant before he could martial his defences. At that moment he was sitting on a stool in the half finished kitchen of his barn conversion also thinking, 'Better watch yourself.'

With autumn came gales and Henry and Marie brought the sheep down into the lower fields for shelter and richer grazing, increasing their ration of feed but not yet needing to supplement with hay. The ram, now separated from the ewes, was back in with the ponies. His thick fleece was impervious to cold and rain but he chose to lie in the warm straw in the calf shed, while the ponies, wrapped in their padded waterproof winter rugs preferred to spend most of their time outside, though they stood close to the stone wall of the building out of the weather.

It was a quiet time on the farm. George came over to walk the fields with Henry, pointing out where hedges needed cutting back and ditches needed clearing before the winter rains could cause flooding, and stayed for supper.

Henry was able to concentrate more on his office work; the project he was engaged in was coming to an end at the close of the year and he was quite looking forward to getting stuck into something new. He expected to be involved in the big contract which they were negotiating and that should prove more interesting than the tedious task of drawing the last one to a conclusion.

Sally was happy at Handy Cross; she walked around the farm, becoming familiar with the sheep and cattle, learning which fields had been harvested for barley and which were sown with winter wheat. There were a couple of farm workers as well as Thomas and Josh and she chatted easily with all of them, and sometimes had a coffee with Ellie in the farmhouse kitchen. These casual relationships suited her, and she still walked over to Holtbourne regularly and occasionally did some pottery with Judith.

When she met Josh there was a guarded friendliness

on both sides,as if there were an unspoken agreement to let things simmer down between them.

Soon after she moved in, he was setting off in the land rover as she was walking down the lane.

'There she is in her new barbour and smart boots, looking every inch the country lady,' he thought with a touch of affectionate amusement.

"Can I give you a lift?"

"Oh, thank you, I'm just going into the village."

She climbed in and suddenly they were both aware of the chemistry between them whenever they were in close proximity.

'It's as if there's a force field around us,' Sally thought, but it no longer concerned her, she knew neither of them was going to disturb the equilibrium.

"Have you thought of getting a cheap car while you're here? It might be worth it just to get about," he observed.

"Actually,I don't drive," she told him.

He was surprised, everyone he knew learned as soon as they got to seventeen, it was a necessity in the country.

"Oh, I see." He didn't know what to make of it. "Did you not want to learn?"

"To be honest, it was never an issue, I have always lived in cities where transport is good and parking is well nigh impossible."

"Oh, I understand, yes of course."

Suddenly he stepped over the invisible line.

"How do you feel about learning now? I could teach you. My mother's old Fiesta is sitting in the garage doing nothing, we could use that."

"Are you sure? That would be wonderful."

'It's a great opportunity, I do need to drive,' she told herself firmly, suppressing the unbidden wave of delight that it was Josh who had asked her. She wasn't going to give that any house room and she was certain the emotion would subside.

Josh was surprised at the warm feeling he got whenever he did anything for Sally. Even something as small as bringing her a load of logs for her fire gave him satisfaction and he left her thinking, ' There, she'll be cosy now when the storage heaters lose power in the evenings.'

He liked to think of her in her bright sitting room when he passed the lighted window in the evenings and hoped she wasn't lonely. Once he had the excuse of arranging the driving lessons he began to pop in sometimes and stayed a while, sharing coffee or a glass of wine. She started offering him supper sometimes and since she was a good cook and even took note of his favourite dishes, it was only natural that he enjoyed her company, or so he told himself.

Sally couldn't pretend she didn't look forward to his visits but she was playing down their significance until Ellie chose to have a word with her about it. She asked Sally in for coffee and warned her off in a pointed way.

"I can't help noticing you and Josh are getting very friendly. You've just come out of a bad relationship. I like you and I don't want to see you get hurt. I've known Josh ever since school and I'm fond of him but he's bad news where women are concerned. It's not that he plays around but he gets involved and then cools off, it's as if he can't commit. One minute it's full steam ahead and then he gets cold feet and it's all off. I've seen it happen to several girls over the years and they've never done anything wrong, he just doesn't want to settle down."

Sally gathered her dignity and she felt a steel trap close over the grief in her heart.

"As you say, I have just got out of a controlling relationship and I'm not looking to get into anything else. I value my freedom too much for that. I like Josh but there's really no more to it than that. Thank you for the heads up though, I know you mean well."

"That's OK then," said Ellie, "Just so long as you know the situation."

Ellie took care to relay Sally's denials to Josh at the first opportunity.

The driving lessons continued but gradually Josh called at the cottage less and not without a genuine reason. Sally was more guarded now though she was always friendly and although Josh was puzzled and a bit hurt, he felt as if a roller coaster he had been on was slowing down and there was an element of relief in that.

'Probably best to cool it for now,' he told himself, following her lead.

Sally spent rather more time away from the farm, joining Judith in the pottery studio or helping Marie make plans for the craft gallery. One day in the run up to Christmas, Marie asked her for a favour.

"Henry's Christmas works do is coming up," she said. "They've been awarded a big new contract and the partners want to push the boat out with a dinner dance in a posh hotel. Henry thinks we should show willing and go and anyway, it'd be a chance to dress up for once. How do you feel about staying over with the kids for the

163

night? They'll still be at school in the day but they can walk down there."

"Of course I will, we can make decorations or something and watch a Christmas movie. We had fun last time I looked after them. If it's before the end of term that's fine. You know I'm going to my brother Paul's with Mum for Christmas. What are you going to wear? "

Marie admired Sally's taste and asked her to come upstairs to help her decide.

Opening the wardrobe she said,

" It comes down to this green dress which I wore last year or the red one which I bought for last year's do but then I didn't have the nerve to wear it."

"Let's have a look then," Sally was in her element. "Try the green dress on."

Marie obeyed, stripping off her jeans and jumper and stepping into the long emerald green gown.

"It's very classy and the colour suits you," Sally said, standing back to get the full effect.

"I have to wear strong colours or I just look sallow," Marie told her.

"OK, now try the other one."

Sally hung the green dress back in the wardrobe while Marie put the flame coloured red dress on.

"Oh, that's the one!" Sally assured her. "You were so right to buy it!"

"It's not too much? I don't want to over do it," Marie was anxious.

"Absolutely not! It's stunning and it's so right for you; it's dramatic but there's nothing flashy about it. Believe me, you look sensational. What about shoes?"

Marie brought a pair of heels out of the wardrobe.

"I know I can dance in these, though they are a bit high."

"Put them on, and put your hair up so we get the full effect."

Marie twisted her hair into a chignon at the back.

"You know, you look a million dollars. Has Henry seen this dress?"

"No, I changed my mind as I said."

"So, don't show him 'til you are ready go out; he'll be the envy of every man in the room, which is what men want of course, and he won't be able to keep his hands off you by the end of the evening."

"Well, that's going to be awkward then," Marie laughed as she peeled the dress off and handed it to Sally, "Because we're staying with his parents. That's a real passion killer. Although come to think of it, their guest room is at the other end of the landing..."

They were both laughing now.

"No problem then, so long as you don't break any furniture."

Guided by their gales of laughter, Henry opened the bedroom door, saying

"What's all this giggling about ?"

He was stopped in his tracks by the unexpected sight of his wife in her underwear, with her hair up, wearing high heels. Sally whisked the red dress back into the wardrobe and then, seeing the look on his face, she slipped past him in the doorway, murmuring,

"I think I'll just put the kettle on."

As Sally went downstairs she felt an unfamiliar hot wave of desire tinged with a little envy and she was distressed to find the feeling was accompanied by an unbidden memory of Josh swinging an axe to chop logs.

Marie and Henry left for their trip to the city in high spirits. It was the first time Marie had been back and it was a novel feeling to be going on an outing together. Chloe had been a bit tearful at being left behind, but Sally had distracted her by offering to help feed the ponies, and they knew the farm was in good hands. It was an advantage that Sally knew their routines from the weeks she had stayed with them.

They arrived at Henry's parents' house in time for tea and after a chat to share news, Marie went upstairs to their rather austere guest room to change. Henry soon followed and was duly impressed  by the red dress.

"This is what you were trying to hide from me that afternoon a couple of weeks ago?" he asked.

"Yes, Sally thought it would have more of an impact if you saw it this evening. But are you sure you like it? It's not too over the top?"

"No, it's fine," he said, pulling on his jacket.
 It wasn't quite the reaction she had been hoping for, but with one more glance in the mirror she followed him downstairs. Of course, his mother had to put a dampener on her evening by remarking,

"Is that what you're wearing dear? You don't think it's a bit obvious? You don't want to stand out too much you know."

It didn't matter how often it happened, her mother in law always had the power to deflate Marie's confidence. This time however she  wasn't prepared to be cowed and replied,

"This evening I intend to see and be seen, there's

some serious networking to be done. We do want Henry to get a leading role with this new contract don't we?"

'I couldn't care less,' Marie thought, 'but it's the way she thinks and it'll take the wind out of her sails for once.'

Arriving at the hotel and being ushered into the function room, Marie pinned a smile on her face and set out to make the evening a success for Henry even if she didn't manage to enjoy it herself. They were greeted by a couple of his colleagues whose partners she had met at other functions. She noticed Amelia's husband Jonathan looked uncomfortable and made a point of talking to him, then someone else approached her whom she hardly recognised and asked after the 'family' because he clearly couldn't remember who her children were. He didn't seem to have his wife with him so she didn't like to reciprocate in case they had separated, but she enthused about the new contract which was a safe subject and on everyone's lips.

Marie noticed several men she didn't know ogling her appreciatively in the red dress and she made her way back to Henry; he might as well get the kudos of having an attractive wife, that was what she was there for after all it seemed.

At that point one of the partners approached them, clapped Henry on the shoulder in a show of bonhomie and asked her how she liked living in the country.

"Very much," she replied, resisting the impulse to tell him that in a month's time she would be spending her nights in a lambing shed doused in ovine amniotic fluid. That would be a conversation stopper she thought.

167

"You must be very busy organising the decorating I suppose. There's so much to do when you move house isn't there?" he asked fatuously.

She wondered if he had been drinking already, and then whether he found these do's as uncomfortable as everyone else and needed some Dutch courage to go round glad handing his staff.

'I'm sure everyone would have welcomed another couple of hundred in their Christmas bonus instead and not had to bother with this charade,' she thought ungraciously.

After that things improved though, perhaps because she was seated quite close to Henry at dinner and they had both had a couple of glasses of rather good wine by then. They exchanged conspiratorial glances which made her feel closer to him and the people immediately surrounding her were relaxing and becoming good fun. One young woman she recognised as being some kind of financial expert for the firm was indiscreet enough to warn her in a penetrating stage whisper to avoid dancing with the other partner who was seated not far away.

" Last year he groped me on the dance floor and I couldn't get away," she said.

Marie glanced in his direction but he seemed engrossed in conversation with someone else.

'Lucky for her,' she thought.

They ended the evening at a table with a couple of Henry's younger colleagues who clearly liked him and looked up to him, which pleased her. She and Henry danced, her cheek on his shoulder oblivious of anyone else, and he was murmuring something into her hair but she couldn't catch what it was. After a while she realised he was singing the romantic song the band was playing and she smiled to herself because normally Henry's singing was pretty bad.

When they got back to Henry's parents' house after a long and very expensive taxi ride, they crept upstairs as quietly as they could. Marie realised that Henry had drunk more than she thought and she had to guide him past the lamp on the landing table which had been left on for their benefit. Closing the bedroom door, he embraced her, more than slightly the worse for wear, saying,

"My lovely wife, in her lovely dress. I love you in this dress, and I love you out of it," trying to remove it. It may not have been the night of passion that Sally envisaged but Marie went home with a happy heart.

They arrived back at Holtbourne to find that Sally had got the children making mince pies, not that there were many left because they had taken some up to the caravan for Lilian and given some to George when he came to check the sheep. They finished the rest over a cup of coffee and even Sally ate two. Marie thought she was looking much better these days, she had lost that air of fragility and had gained a few pounds which suited her.

# Chapter 12

Soon preparations for Christmas were in full swing;
Marie's parents were coming and they wanted to make
the first celebration in their new home special. They
prevailed on George to join them for Christmas dinner;
he hesitated at first, saying,

"No,no, you've got family coming," but when he
heard it was only Marie's parents, he accepted.

He had met them before and found them easy to talk
to. Marie had worried about Lilian being on her own,
although she didn't know her, but Sally told her Lilian's
idea of Christmas lunch was a game stew simmered on
top of her stove and a warming shot of sloe gin to go
with it. Jack was despatched back up the hill on
Christmas Eve though with more mince pies and some
home made  shortbread.

Hearing that Sally was going away for Christmas,
Josh insisted on taking her to the station and meeting her
when  she came back.

"You can drive to Taunton, it'll be good practice for
you."

"Really? I'm not used to driving in a lot of traffic."

"You'll be fine," he told her. "You don't have to go
right through town to get to the station and anyway
you'll have to take your test there so you'd better get
used to it."

In the last few weeks they had been careful around
each other, attentive and considerate, but both aware that

the other had taken a step back.

On the way to Taunton Josh talked very little, letting Sally concentrate on her driving. He directed her to the short stay area in front of the station where it was easy to pull in and carried her case into the entrance hall although she said she could manage. Waiting while she got her ticket out of the machine, he realised he didn't want to see her go, even for a short while. What if her family persuaded her to move closer to them?

'Well she'll be back for New Year whatever happens,' he told himself.

She bent to pick up her case, turned to thank him for the lift and they hesitated, neither of them wanting to part.

"Happy Christmas Josh," she said, making a half move towards him.

At once he reached for her, a lingering bear hug and a kiss on the cheek; rapt in that moment each was aware of the the scent and feel of the other, encumbered as they were by jackets and scarves.

Josh watched as she passed through the glass doors, passengers only, and went up the steps to the platform, struggling a little with the case so she did not turn back. His emotional confusion driving back to the farm was matched only by hers as she gazed unseeing out of the train window while the countryside slipped past.

Sally hadn't spent Christmas with her brother since she was at university when they had both gone home to their mother's house. Paul was married now, with a baby son, and he wanted to host the festivities. Fortunately, his wife came from a large family and was unfazed by visitors, letting them take over the kitchen while she looked after the baby.

Sally and her mother had talked in depth on her last visit and now they bonded over the turkey, laughing and chatting as they prepared the vegetables, using family recipes for bread sauce and stuffings. It was a happy, busy few days but in the end Sally was glad to board the train again and head back to the West Country.

Josh was waiting at the back of the station, ready to take her case and hold the car door open for her.

"You're driving home," he announced, so again conversation was limited until they were well clear of the town. She asked how he had spent Christmas day. He had enjoyed the day with Thomas and Ellie, helping the boys assemble a complicated car race track and popping out to do essential chores for the animals.

"If you have stock they have to come first, whatever else is going on."

"Yes, of course. Did you see your mother?"

"She came over with her partner Frank on Boxing Day, he's a nice guy,easy going, you know."

"It's good that you all get on. I think Thomas mentioned your Mum had remarried."

"Thomas may well have said that, I think he's a bit embarrassed that they're not actually married. Lots of older people don't bother with all that these days do they, especially when there's property and children on both sides. Mum met Frank when she joined a U3A group and they really get on. They live in his bungalow in Minehead but she often comes over to help out with the boys; he never minds, he's got family of his own after all."

"I think that sounds ideal," she said. "I wish my mother would meet someone. Your mother must have been devastated when your Dad died so suddenly."

"It was a shock and she took a while to get over it," he said diplomatically, and glancing sideways at his face she saw the enigmatic expression she associated with emotional withdrawal. Maybe it wasn't such a happy marriage, she wondered, that might explain quite a lot.

"Mum and Frank are having the boys over New Year. We're going to the pub, do you want to come?"

"I said I'd go round to the Hall first and go with Sophie and Jed and that crowd."

"OK, there's no point in getting there 'til half nine or so. We'll be walking down, so make sure you come back with us, you don't want to be wandering about late on your own, there'll be some drunks about."

"Thank you, I'll see you there anyway."

They parked the Fiesta and went their separate ways.

"I put the heating on for you," he called as she opened her door.

The cottage did feel warm and welcoming and she was glad to be home, however temporary that was. That evening Sally got the tarot cards out and for the first time in a year she did a spread for herself. She hadn't wanted to face what she knew the cards would reveal before; she knew it was less a revelation of the future as a fixed destiny, but more a way of harnessing her own intuition and will. Now she felt ready to engage with her future and discern a way forward, although there were no fixed points on her horizon.

She asked, "What will the next year bring?"

The first card was the six of swords, denoting a move

away from a stormy past, releasing baggage, a transition. Well, she felt she had achieved that at last. The second card was the four of wands, indicating a new, secure, happy home. That was very reassuring. She was surprised by the third card, the Ace of Cups. She sat and stared at it for a while, hope and doubt conflicting in her mind. Finally she had to admit that if it was a card someone else had drawn she would have interpreted it in only one way; new emotional connections, a new relationship.

'So, who knows,' she thought, 'enough has changed in the last year, I guess anything can happen.'

The first Christmas in their new home was a happy one for the Freemans. Marie's parents arrived with a car full of food and presents and kept the children occupied playing new board games and scalextric. They were easy guests and although Henry and Marie collapsed on the sofa after waving them off, there was real regret at seeing them go. Marie and the children missed the casual almost daily contact they had enjoyed before and she was a bit tearful as she kissed her parents goodbye.

"They can come back whenever they like, you know that. They're always welcome," Henry said, trying to comfort her.

They weren't on their own for long because Henry's older sister Margaret was staying for the first time, over New Year. They rarely saw her because of her highly successful career as a barrister in London and recently they had only met on her rare visits to their parents. Chloe was the first to spot the Mercedes sports car turning in to the drive.

"Auntie Maggs, Auntie Maggs," she cried, rushing to the door.

Henry's sister had inherited the family height but it lent a slightly angular look to her slim frame. She was sleek and stylish, like an Afghan hound Marie always thought, but without the flowing locks; in fact her dark hair was cut to collar length in a chic bob.

"Darlings,"she embraced the children first,"Look at you, how you've grown!"

Henry carried her luggage into the hall, going back for several mysterious parcels all beautifully wrapped. Margaret could be relied on to make the best of anything.

"What a journey," she said. "You certainly are in the sticks out here. The A303 was a nightmare. The sat nav was useless, I don't think I'd have found you at all but I asked a funny little man in a woolly hat down at the bungalows and he knew exactly where you were."

"That funny little man is our very good friend George," Henry told her, "And without him I don't think we'd have got the place off the ground."

"Well I'm glad you found a good handyman or whatever he is," she replied. "If mother is to be believed, you've certainly got your work cut out."

He let it go at that.

Margaret was generous and she chose her presents imaginatively, so the children couldn't wait to open their parcels. Both children had Pelham puppets, Chloe a pony and a princess, Jack had a knight and a dragon.

"That's amazing! I remember those from our childhood, I didn't know they still made them!"

" I thought they were old enough not to get them into

such a tangle. You remember the state ours used to get into,"she said.

"I do indeed, and it made Mum mad because she had to sort the strings out. I wonder what happened to ours?"

"Chucked out long ago I expect, Mother was never sentimental about our things was she? The other presents are more practical though."

Chloe was delighted with her chocolate coloured jodhpurs with a lilac stripe down the outside leg and holding up a riding jacket she exclaimed,

"Oh, it's Musto, Tamsin has one of these, wait 'til I show her!"

She wore the jods for the rest of the day.

The most successful present however was Jack's night vision binoculars. For some minutes he was speechless, examining them and reading the leaflet, then he got up and put his arms round Margaret as she sat in her chair, hugging her and kissing her cheek, an unusual spontaneous gesture from a ten year old boy.

He simply said, "Auntie Maggs, you're the best."

"Well that seems to have gone down well," she said with satisfaction. "I could do with a drink."

Marie remembered that Margaret drank rather more than she ate and went to open a bottle of wine from the box Henry had brought in from the car. She noticed it also contained a fine single malt; obviously Margaret was taking no chances with their choice of supermarket plonk.

There was plenty of food left from Christmas so a cold buffet was followed at dinner time by a turkey and gammon pie. Margaret had the tour of the farm, gingerly stepping through the mud in unsuitable soft leather boots and after the children had gone up to bed, (or in Jack's case to hang out of the window trying out his binoculars), the grown ups opened the doors of the wood burner and settled down for the evening.

After exchanging general news, Marie was yawning and decided to leave brother and sister to it, a rare opportunity for a proper catch up. The end of a year encourages reflection and Margaret was nursing her whisky in a mellow mood.

"So how is my little brother really? The parents are full of dire predictions but that's not new. Is it working out for you, this farming lark?"

"To be honest, I don't know yet whether we can make a go of it financially, but while I'm still doing the day job we can keep our heads above water. We love this life though, I can't wait to get the poly tunnels up and start growing things. That's my real passion and apart from the veg patch I haven't had the chance to get stuck into it yet. The children are thriving as you see. Chloe is so into horses now I can't imagine depriving her of that and as to Jack, he's just immersed in it; not so much farming itself but the landscape and wild life."

"Yes, I noticed that when we were going round the place, he's quite intense isn't he? I suppose Chloe can train as a vet, there's no money in horses as such, as far as I can gather from colleagues with horse mad daughters, but Jack could be an environmentalist, maybe he could host TV shows or something."

Trust Margaret to have ambitious plans for them.

"And how about you, what do you do when you aren't in court?"

"When I'm not in court I'm generally conning briefs

or consulting with solicitors or clients. It's a pretty closed world the inns of court, and it's pretty dog eat dog because we're all in competition but we socialise of course. It's very adversarial though, but I'm good at that."

"I know you are," he smiled. "I grew up with you, remember? But what about a personal life, there's no man on the horizon these days?"

"Oh, I may as well tell you. There is someone from another chambers but he's married and he's never going to leave his wife. To be honest, I'm not sure it would work out if he did. It's been going on for years but we're very discreet. He has a secret hideaway in Tuscany and we go there for the odd weekend."

"His wife doesn't know about this Italian place?" Henry was incredulous. "How does he explain being away?"

"That's easy, we all work away a lot, and with mobile phones, or even face time, you could be anywhere."

"Would you not like a proper relationship though, seriously? What about children, it 's not too late."

"I know, and I have thought about it, but can you see me with a baby? A few years ago I actually considered having a child, maybe even by donor to keep it simple, but the poor little thing would be fobbed off with nannies all the time and what sort of life is that? I envy you and Marie in some ways, you're great together and the kids are a joy, but I have made my life and I'm not suited to anything else."

On that note they parted for the night, with Henry feeling sorry for his sister for the first time in his life. Marie was half awake when he went up and he wanted to share his thoughts.

"I don't know if she's the product of nature or nurture," he told her. "When our parents realised how bright she was they would be on her like hawks to fulfil all their ambitions, but maybe that competitive spirit was in her to start with."

"She's doing alright anyway," was all Marie could muster, snuggling into his chest. " I'm glad she felt close enough to confide in you."

While the Freemans opened a bottle of champagne at home, most of the younger  locals headed for The Plough. Marie had suggested Henry take his sister to the pub for a while but neither of them thought that was a good idea.

Sally went down with a group from the Hall who had started drinking early and were already merry. The bar was crowded and they had to force their way through the throng to find standing room. The speakers were pumping out music and it was hard to make conversation so Sally bought a bottle of wine at the bar to share with Sophie and Jed the blacksmith  who seemed to be on his own that evening, and stuck with them. Hannah had taken her little daughter away to join her partner who was working over the holiday.

Ellie was at the other side of the bar with Thomas and Josh who had his back to her, but when Ellie waved and beckoned to Sally to join them, she just waved back, not wanting to leave Sophie on her own to keep Jed company since he seemed determined to drink himself into oblivion. She looked round for the rest of the group from the Hall but couldn't locate them in the crowd.

Sally had another drink but found she stayed clear headed; this wasn't her favourite way to spend an evening and she was feeling quite detached when the landlord turned the music off and tuned the giant TV, usually reserved for football coverage, for the run up to midnight. Sally watched as celebrities contributed their sound bites, the MC shouted ever more enthusiastically and finally the skirl of the pipes brought them up to midnight.

As the countdown began, Sally noticed Josh was making his way through the crowd towards her and at the stroke of midnight when everyone turned to their neighbours, Josh pulled her into his arms and kissed her. It wasn't a drunken embrace; at first he brushed his lips with hers and as she responded, kissed her deeply, so tenderly that her senses reeled and she didn't even think about coming up for air. She felt the warmth of his muscled back through his shirt and for a moment they stood together in a charmed circle until Thomas who had been drinking steadily came up and threw a clumsy arm round his brother's shoulder saying,

"Happy New Year Josh, me old mucker," in a slurred voice.

Ellie came over to intervene and the moment, whatever it meant,was lost. Ellie hugged first Sally and then Josh, wishing them each a Happy New Year, apparently unaware that they had interrupted anything more than the usual round of good wishes. Sophie kissed Sally, Jed hugged everyone whether he knew them or not and Thomas dragged Josh back to the bar to get another drink.

Someone started a conga and by the time that was

over Sally began to wonder if she had read more into the encounter than Josh had intended.

People were starting to think about going home and this time when Ellie waved to her, Sally made her way over to them.

"You're walking back with us aren't you?" Ellie was shepherding her flock and ushering them to the door. For most of the walk back Ellie was talking animatedly to Sally while trying to keep Thomas on his feet. At one point Josh came up on her other side and took Sally's arm, pointing with his flash light and saying,

"Careful, there's black ice here," but he then left her, to help Ellie keep Thomas upright.

Back at the farm, it was obvious the cold night air had done nothing to sober Thomas up and Josh went into the farmhouse with Ellie, all of them calling Good Night and Happy New Year to Sally as she entered the quiet sanctuary of her cottage alone.

She didn't know what to make of the evening but she could still feel the warm pressure of Josh's firm lips on hers and the feel of his palms caressing her back. As she got into bed she was filled with a mixture of doubt, hope and longing, but next morning everything seemed to have returned to the way it was before and she determined not to dwell on it. It must have been an impulse, people let their hair down at New Year after all.

She didn't know that after helping Ellie get Thomas upstairs to bed, Josh spent some minutes standing in the cold outside her door, struggling with indecision. If he had seen a light on he would have knocked and the evening would have ended very differently; as it was, he went back to his half-finished house which was cheerless despite the underfloor heating. The unfurnished shell of the sitting room seemed particularly unwelcoming and the kitchen lacked warmth and character because he had not settled on a colour scheme for the tiles, so there was nothing for it but to retreat upstairs past the closed doors of more unfinished rooms to his bachelor bedroom.

'I must get this house finished,' he thought, 'it's as cold and empty as my heart.' In fact his heart was full, but it was frozen.

Before she left, Margaret took Henry to one side and insisted on giving him a generous cheque, saying,

"This is for the poly tunnels. If this is your dream, I want you to be able to give it your best shot, without having to compromise on the project. Go for it, I'd really love to see you succeed."

"You can't give me all this Maggs, it's too much."

"I'll be very upset if you don't cash it. I can afford it and I can't think of any better use for the money. You can send me some pics when it's up and running."

Henry accepted the gift and hugged his sister with gratitude; he had been trying to work out how to cut the set up costs.

"I've always believed in you, you know," she told him. "Have some faith in yourself !"

# Chapter 13

The Christmas period had been chilly and wet at times, but as George warned them, real winter on Exmoor usually comes towards the end of January. So it was that when Marie received a text to say that lambing was underway at Handy Cross, it was virtually cold enough for her hand to freeze to the metal gate when she entered the farm yard at the back of the house.

All the ewes which had been scanned in lamb had been brought in to two long modern barns with fluorescent light and water laid on. Those not due immediately had access to an outside area, since close confinement encouraged infections to spread, but the early ewes were in a closed barn with many small individual pens set up along the sides which each housed a new mother and her lambs. Thomas was doing a day shift with one of the farm hands, Colin, and he called her over immediately to see her first lamb born.

"We're really getting under way now," he told her, "so you can get plenty of practice if you muck in."

She was only too keen to learn and the hours passed quickly, her ears filled with the bleating of the ewes and their lambs, and the constant activity keeping them all busy. She was used to handling sheep of course and the smell of their fleeces was nothing new, but the sheer size of the flock with all the massed bodies in a confined space was almost overwhelming at first.

The job itself was both repetitive and challenging.

Most ewes gave birth easily, the lambs slipping out onto the straw to be rubbed down and encouraged to breathe, a wisp of hay clearing their nostrils, watched to see that they were strong enough to stand and that the ewe allowed them to suckle. If there were twins they would each be smaller, and sometimes one would be weaker and need encouragement to feed. The young two tooth ewes occasionally rejected their lambs and that was where the individual pens came into their own. Not only could a lamb not wander off and be lost but its mother could not abandon it. As a last resort, a ewe could be tethered to the wooden partition by one leg so that she couldn't circle to throw off the lamb until she accepted it and got into the habit of allowing it to suckle. That was rare, however, the maternal instinct was strong and bonding usually needed no encouragement.

At first Marie did routine tasks like refilling the water buckets in each pen which was a regular job since they were small and only filled half way so that a lamb could not get soaked in cold water or even drown. She checked the ewes and alerted the men if one went into labour, rubbing down the newborns and making sure that they were on their feet and suckling. Extra eyes observing the flock were welcome and her calm way of carrying the lambs to lead their dams to a pen saved extra work for the experienced lambers.

"D'you want to check the ones under the lights?" Thomas asked and she went over to a pen in a sheltered corner where those who were too weak to suckle by themselves or the few which were orphaned, lay in a huddle under lights to keep them warm. At first the weak ones had to be bottle fed at least every six hours, day and night but as they got stronger they could suckle from a shepherdess bucket whenever they wanted. This ingenious contraption had a double skin so that water kept at just the right temperature warmed the milk bucket in which teats were fixed so that a lamb could drink at will.

Marie bottle fed a couple of the tiniest, her own maternal instincts stirred as she sat in the straw cradling the little body with its crisp close wool coat under her arm, tilting the bottle with its long teat at just the right angle to avoid air bubbles as you would for a human baby, and noting how much each had taken.

A rough table stood near the entrance to the barn with a cracked sink and kettles to heat water to dissolve the milk powder and here she made coffee to hand out to the men, standing by with her mug watching as they dealt with a difficult birth.

"You see, this lamb has only one foreleg come out," Colin explained, "The other is folded inside, so you have to put your hand in and ease the lamb back so you can straighten the other leg out . There, you see, it slips out easily now."

"What would happen if she lambed by herself in the field?" Marie asked.

"It'd never be born," Thomas told her, "It'd die inside her and eventually she'd get an infection and die too. We lose some ewes anyway, even with antibiotics, if they get an infection after the birth. If they die on the second or third day you get orphan lambs and have to rear them in the pen over there, unless you can get another ewe with a singleton to adopt them. If they're just weak you can often put them back onto the ewe."

At the end of the shift, Marie drove home tired but elated.

'I can do this with my own flock,' she thought, 'I'm getting a feel for it.'

It wasn't until she got out of the car that she realised how filthy she was and how badly she smelt. Henry had walked down to pick the children up from school but there was no-one in the kitchen as she passed through.

"Just going for a shower," she called as she made for the stairs.

'I'm going to have to wash my hair every day at this rate,' she thought, 'And these clothes have got to go straight in the machine.'

"So how was it?" Henry asked her, over the sausage and mash supper he had cooked. He had been working in the office all day and was beginning to realise that the next few weeks were going to be full on for him too.

"It's just busy all the time, so many animals to look after, so much going on. They've got over two hundred ewes to lamb over four weeks. Thomas and Josh do a twelve hour shift pretty much every day, Ellie does some day shifts, and I think Colin and Roger take it in turns to do days or nights and then there are some part-timers when they're in the thick of it for the next fortnight or three weeks. They seem very organised though and there's a roster. Thomas has suggested I work four day shifts this week and then some night work which they'll pay quite good money for. It'll take some organising this end, but we knew that and we'll know in advance what I'm doing."

"We can manage for a few weeks whatever it takes,"

Henry assured her. "We could do with the money and anyway, you need the practice."

"I certainly do, but I can see that you can't just leave ewes to get on with it, there can be difficult births and I wouldn't forgive myself if I lost any because I wasn't around."

"We'll cross that bridge when we come to it. If it's a case of going out and checking them at night I can take a turn and only call you if there's a problem."

"I can do that too Mum," Jack offered.

"Me too," said Chloe.

"Well, we'll see Darlings, it's good to know I have so many willing helpers."

Marie was grateful to have her family behind her, but she couldn't envisage her small daughter trotting out to the barn alone in the dark.

The next weeks were hectic for Marie, combining her usual chores with long shifts at Handy Cross but she learned invaluable lessons. She learned to cope with difficult births herself under supervision, earning praise for her dexterity in  drawing a bent leg forward. Once during a night shift Josh even asked her to try turning a lamb slightly to bring the head forward in the pelvis.

"Its nose is up and it's a tight fit, smaller hands might help," he said. "Push it back and try turning the shoulders and head to the left. Yes, you've got it, proper job, as Roger would say," as the lamb slipped out. "It's flat and dehydrated though, we'll have to tube it."

Josh swung the lamb by its legs to get it breathing.

"It looks harsh but it works," he told her. She watched as he sat it up against his knees.

"You see, he's breathing now but his head lolls back, that's how you know he's dehydrated so we have to get some fluid into him. We can pass some colostrum formula down a tube directly into his stomach, down his throat like this so it doesn't go into his lungs."

She definitely wouldn't be confident to do that she thought. It did the trick though and after an hour the lamb was on its feet and before the end of her shift it was suckling from the ewe.

'Not a small miracle' she thought. 'Being a shepherd takes years of experience and you never stop learning. If I can be half as good I'll be proud.'

When Marie was doing a night shift, Sally sometimes came into the barn in the evening with cake or home made cookies to hand round and stopped to fill the water buckets or make up formula and feed any lambs which needed a bottle. She seemed to know who was on the rota though, Marie noticed, because she never came in if Josh was there.

Of course, Marie had long since realised that something was going on between Sally and Josh and their on – off courtship was a puzzle to her. She had seen them exchange longing glances or talk animatedly and apparently at ease, while at other times, like now, they seemed to be avoiding one another. She knew better than to ask Sally, she would tell her when she was ready. One evening Sally miscalculated though and Josh appeared in the doorway, saying he had swapped with Colin. An open tin of Sally's cookies lay on the table and he asked,

"Has Sally been in then?"

"She's bottle feeding," Marie told him, curious to see how he would react.

He went over to the pen but she couldn't gather what passed between them. After some minutes he came past, helped himself to a cookie and crossed to the other side of the barn to check on the ewes gathered in the open section. Eventually Sally emerged, said goodnight and left, leaving Marie none the wiser. How annoying.

As lambing at Handy Cross dwindled to the last few, Marie was laid off and life returned to something like normality at Holtbourne. She was exhausted by the long shifts doing heavy work and could only imagine how Colin and Roger felt who were both middle aged; her own back and shoulders ached and she was young. In a few weeks they would be into calving and although there were not so many cows, it would all start again for them. Henry was relieved, saying,

"I really must get up to the office, I've put it off as it is. I've got to meet one of the partners for my annual review and no-one looks forward to that. To be honest I've been leaving site visits to the younger guys more than I should."

"Will it be Mr. Smarmy or Mr. Gropey?" she asked facetiously.

"Don't be mean!" but he was amused. "I don't know yet but I've finished the project I was on, the report's gone in and I've just been doing the usual explaining the findings and justifying the recommendations, you know how it works. I'll be finding out what part they want me to play in this big new contract. At least that will be more interesting."

Henry was grateful that he had been able to coast through the last few weeks and he had enough to think about with ordering the poly tunnels and researching what varieties of peppers, melons and squashes to grow, but as he drove up the motorway, the usual switch kicked in and he got into city mode. With that buzz of adrenaline he felt he was up for a work challenge.

He had got into the habit of catching up with his two young colleagues as soon as he got into the office. They could be relied on to get him up to speed with office politics and any undercurrents he may have missed. He sensed a more purposeful air about the place and everyone seemed to be in a hurry. He spotted one unfamiliar face, and he didn't look like a junior.

'Ah, they've been recruiting then,' he thought.

"So what have I missed?" he perched on the corner of Jason's desk, coffee in hand.

"We're gearing up for the big contract. They've identified the various projects and are setting up teams, one of them is being led by the new golden boy, he's been head hunted from Fishers and they're spitting feathers."

"I see," Henry vaguely recognised him now. He wanted to ask if Jason had heard what role he was to play himself but that would be demeaning; he would have to wait for his meeting for that. At three o'clock he went up to the partners' office.

'Oh, it's Mr. Smarmy,' remembering Marie's jibe took the edge off his nerves.

"Ah, Henry, have a seat." He was being expansive. "I'm glad we have the opportunity for this discussion. How are things going in your new home? Settled in now?"

"Very well, thank you, yes, we like it."

"So you see this as a permanent move then?"

Henry was surprised.

"Yes, we've bought a house with some land," he took care never to refer to it as a farm.

"The thing is, we feel you have become somewhat, how can I put this, detached from us here. I used to rely on you for lateral thinking, a creative and innovative approach but that seems to be lacking now, you seem to be less engaged. I wonder how you feel about that."

"We've just concluded the project I was on, are you not happy with that?"

"That was pretty mundane stuff, a bread and butter contract and yes, the client is satisfied. Nevertheless, I think you have taken your eye off the ball a bit and we can't afford to let things slide. We're expanding and we all have to be focused. This new contract is very exciting and puts us firmly in the lead."

"It is exciting," Henry was trying to sound enthusiastic, "And I'm looking forward to contributing to that."

"There are going to be many elements to draw together, a lot of liaison between teams and we can't afford to let anything get missed. Not to mention the client contact, much of that has to be site visits of course. Communication is going to be vital and I'm afraid it's too nuanced to risk anyone being out of the loop. We have decided to give you something you can manage more safely if you're working from home. It's a smaller project but equally important to our reputation, I want you to handle the Masons contract, you can lead on that and have Jason and Adam to assist you."

Henry knew his young colleagues would be bitterly disappointed to be left out of the more prestigious contract; streamlining an old fashioned family firm to make it marketable had no kudos and wouldn't enhance their career prospects.

Henry kept much to himself in the next couple of days, making him feel even more isolated in the office. He set up a working schedule with Jason and Adam who were in fact given more responsibility than they would have had as junior members of a bigger team; perhaps it wouldn't look too bad on their CVs after all. It was pedestrian work for someone with his experience though and driving home Henry had a sense of foreboding.

'They're not wrong,' he had to admit. 'My heart isn't in it any more.'

Explaining the situation to Marie later he said,

"To be honest if I can hang on there for another two years it's all I can expect. We have to make the farm turn a profit. I know it won't happen this year but we have to make it pay the year after. I hope the craft gallery is a success, I think we have to pin our hopes on that to make a major contribution."

Marie was doing her best to get on with it.


Sally was sitting in her cottage at ten o'clock one evening, wearing the black kimono she used as a dressing gown when she heard a commotion in the courtyard. The farm dogs were barking and a car door slammed. She got up to draw back the curtain, wondering what was going on and was horrified to see Matthew getting out of his car, and staring straight at her as she was silhouetted by the light from the window. She closed the curtain but it was too late,the next moment he was hammering with his fist on the door yelling,

"Sally, open the door, I want to talk to you, you bitch!"

Sally shrank back against the sofa, overwhelmed by terror. All the persecution, the hold he had over her and the scene at her mother's flat came flooding back.
He came round and knocked on the window, shouting,

"I know you're in there. Let me in! Open that door now!"

Then everything happened at once. The dogs were barking under her window and there were several raised voices. She couldn't resist peeping out and saw that the house door had opened with the family grouped in the doorway, Thomas in front holding a shotgun, Ellie behind him and the boys craning their necks to see. All the yard lights had come on and the scene was illuminated brightly now.

"Who the hell are you?" Thomas was angry."What do you want?"

By now Josh had pulled on a leather jerkin and come across the yard to confront Matthew, quelling the dogs' clamour with a command.

"You can get back in your car now and get out of here, the lady wants nothing to do with you," he said coldly.

"Out of my way, it's none of your business," Matthew said, and turned to pick up a pot full of geraniums to hurl at the window.

"You've made me homeless you stupid cow," he shouted. "I've lost the flat and the bailiffs have got all your precious furniture, what do you think of that?"

He raised the pot but dropped it with a crash when Josh grabbed him by the elbow and spun him round to face him.

" I'm making it my business," he insisted calmly.
" You can get back in your car and leave now."

"Are you going to do something ?" Ellie was asking
Thomas.

"My brother seems to be enjoying himself", Thomas
said. "He doesn't need any help from me."

"Ah, I see how it is," Matthew sneered. "She's got
you under her spell now has she Farm Boy? Think she'll
stay with you? She'll be off back to her university friends
and her scientists. She's too good for you, she's only
using you."

For a moment Josh was cut to the quick and the
impulse to punch Matthew in the mouth to shut him up
nearly overcame him, but long years of living with his
father had taught him to control his temper.

"She's too good for you, that's for sure," he replied.

Matthew was provoked and made a lunge at Josh,
setting the dogs barking again, but Josh was too quick
for him, tripping him with a classic soccer foul so that he
landed heavily on the tarmac. Matthew struggled to his
feet; winded and surrounded by growling dogs he started
to back off.

Josh took a dominant stance, like the stags he had
watched so often during the rut and when he spoke it
was with deliberate chilling malice.

"If I see you anywhere near this farm again, I'll let the
dogs have you and when they've finished I'll put you
through the grinder and feed you to the pigs. There'll be
nothing left. Now get in your car and go back where you
came from. Get off my land!"

Matthew retreated to the car, swearing. Once safely

in the driving seat his bravado returned and he revved the engine loudly. Thomas raised the shot gun and Josh stepped aside, both apprehensive that Matthew would try to run Josh down, but he turned the car with a screech of brakes, driving through the gates so fast he scarcely made the corner into the lane. They stood and watched his tail lights disappear down the hill before Thomas came over and clapped Josh on the shoulder.

"That was a good tackle Bro, I haven't seen you do that since Young Farmers. And what was all that about feeding him to the pigs, for Gods sake we don't even keep pigs!"

He was laughing, a release of the tension they both felt. Josh was still gritting his teeth.

"No idea, must have seen it in a movie," he muttered. Thomas marshalled his family back into the house.

"The excitement's over for one night boys, better get to bed, there's school tomorrow."

"Why was that man yelling at poor Sally?" asked Ryan.

"If that was her ex, he's a loser," was Sean's considered opinion.

"I'd better go and see if Sally's alright," Ellie offered.

"No, leave it to Josh, he's earned the right to follow this up I reckon."

"If he can make his mind up," she answered darkly. "I've never known anyone like your brother for sitting on the fence."

When Josh tapped on the cottage door, Sally opened it, white faced and trembling with shock. He stepped inside, shutting the door behind him and took her in his arms to comfort her. She was crying silently, her tears

195

making a damp patch on his shoulder and he held her quietly,stroking her hair and back, murmuring softly,

"It's alright sweetheart, he won't be back, that's the end of it now."

He was becoming all too aware of her soft roundness under the light fabric and desire flared unbidden as so often happened in her presence. The thought came that it would be natural to take her now, to possess and protect her, she needed a strong man to look after her, but he knew that would be another instance of taking advantage now that she was vulnerable. She didn't need another man to take over her life.

As her tears subsided she drew away, saying,

" Sorry you had to go through all that. I must apologise to Thomas and Ellie in the morning."

He guided her to sit down on the sofa and hunkered down in front of her.

"No need, they understand and I rather enjoyed myself. Like all bullies, he's a coward, he won't bother you again. Let me make you a cup of tea, you're all in."

Josh made her a mug of tea but didn't trust himself to stay to watch her drink it. He was reminded of the day she moved in and how struck he had been by her beauty. His feelings had deepened since then and now she had melted his heart.

"Try to get some sleep, you're safe here and the dogs are always on guard."

She rose to see him out; he ran his thumb over her face where the tears had dried, moving a curl back into place and kissed her lightly on the cheek.

"Goodnight Sweetheart," he said as he walked out into the dark. "Lock your door now."

Next morning Sally woke late to sunlight streaming through her window and was surprised to find she had slept well. She was feeling calm, as if a great weight had been lifted. The chaotic scene at her mother's home when no-one had been able to stand up to Matthew was replaced by his complete humiliation by Josh. She ceased to see him as a powerful monster but rather as the pathetic blustering failure he was. She felt liberated and a new resolution was forming as she dressed and put on her make up.

She walked over to Holtbourne, suddenly keen to consult Marie. As they sat in her friend's welcoming kitchen, she related   the events of last night.

"Josh was amazing,"she said, "Completely in charge of the situation. He didn't give Matthew an inch and Matthew just backed down and left. I really think I'm free of him forever at last. You know, it was always painful unfinished business 'til now."

"Well, that's a great result." Marie was delighted. "And Josh really defended you; that shows how much he cares."

"Yes, I think he does care for me in a way, but I know he has commitment issues. He's too honourable to mess me  about. Neither of us wants a casual affair so that's a stalemate and anyway I'm not at all sure I should be thinking about another relationship now. The thing is, it's time I moved on with my life. I have to leave the cottage in April because they have bookings from Easter and although I love Exmoor I can't see any point in looking for a cottage to rent in one of the other villages. I feel at home right here but if I was five miles away I might as well be anywhere. There's a job advertised in Manchester which would be a step up for me career wise and it's in a field I know, so I think I stand a chance of getting it. I've been putting off applying but I'm going to do it and see what happens."

"Do you know anyone in Manchester?"

"No, but it's a really vibrant city with a lot going on. It'd be a completely fresh start."

Marie could see why Sally was thinking of making a drastic move, after all the whole Exmoor experience was only meant to be a stop gap while she sorted herself out. She was disappointed though, particularly because she could see there was a real connection between Sally and Josh, but somehow they kept missing the mark. 'Someone should knock their heads together,' she thought crossly.

Later in the day Josh knocked on the cottage door and asked Sally to come over to the barn conversion for a coffee.

"I've got a favour to ask," he said.

This was a first, she had never been invited in before, it was very much his private domain.

"Of course, anything I can do," and she followed him across the court yard into the spacious kitchen which was now virtually complete.

She looked around with interest, admiring the black granite work surfaces which toned with large grey and white patterned floor tiles and contrasted with gleaming white cupboards. He made filter coffee while she perched on a stool. Twin Neff ovens caught her attention and she made some remark about them; she was surprised at the quality of all the fittings, he had put a lot of effort into the design so far.

"The only thing that's been cooked in those ovens up to now is pizza," he admitted ruefully. "Let me show you round and I'll tell you what the problem is."

Josh led her from room to room, a large empty sitting room with views over the fields, square hall with a front door, currently never used, opening onto the courtyard. There was a downstairs cloakroom, wide polished wooden stairs which matched the flooring, two bedrooms which were still unfurnished, a bathroom and the large master with en suite. She felt uncomfortable when he opened his bedroom door and she glimpsed his big bed with its masculine black leather headboard, but he led her past the bank of built in wardrobes with mirrored doors straight into the en suite, explaining,

"I've so nearly finished the place, all the fixtures are in, but it's soulless, I haven't a clue how to finish it. I know you've got good taste, what do you think about tiles? All these rooms need some colour don't they?"

She agreed with that. They went from room to room discussing colours and she lost the feeling of awkwardness, becoming involved with the project in hand. Back in the kitchen over another coffee she said,

" You need some warmth in here, a deep sunflower yellow or maybe better still a Tuscan or Moroccan red."

"I knew you'd have some ideas," he said. " How about coming to Exeter with me on Saturday? I've found a good tile place online. You could help me choose and I'll treat us to lunch. If we take the Fiesta, you can drive, you haven't had much practice while we were lambing."

"Yes, I'd like that," Sally told him, "it's a lovely house, it deserves finishing properly."

"I'm glad you like it," he said.

Their day out was light hearted and fun. They spent ages in the tile showroom but arrived at some unusual and attractive choices, and then went to a good Italian restaurant for lunch, which someone had recommended to Josh.

"This is nice," said Sally, appreciatively. She was glad to sit down and relax after an intense morning.

"You deserve a good bottle of Barolo at least," Josh told her, "but that will have to wait since we're driving."

They chose Elderflower presse instead and settled down to enjoy their lunch. By the time they got back to the multi storey the sky was overcast and as she drove homewards Sally had to put the headlights on.

It was dark in the car, they were both tired and fell into a relaxed intimate silence. At last Josh started to speak.

"There's something I'd like to try to explain to you," he said.

"Hmmm..." she made encouraging noises.

"This isn't meant to be an excuse for the way I've been, but I want you to understand."

"Ok," she said softly.

"Our father wasn't a violent man, though he had a temper, I don't want you to get the wrong idea. He got on fine with Thomas, he was bigger, tougher, held his own and Dad respected him for that. I was quite small as a child and I never matched up to his expectations of what his son should be. He was trying to get me to man up I suppose, but what happened was that I just clammed up when he was around and that seemed to irritate him more. I think he took it for defiance. I won't go on about it, but for instance when I was fifteen I spent my Christmas money and all my savings on a guitar. I'd had an old one but this was a good make, a Fender, and I was very pleased with it. He heard me playing in my room one day and thought I hadn't done my chores; actually I had but that was beside the point. He had a go at me and ended up throwing it on the floor and ruining it. I think he was sorry afterwards, at least Mum said he was, but it was over a year before I bothered to replace it. He'd spoiled it for me then."

"I'm so sorry," Sally said, "That's horrible."

"What I want to say is I think that the way I grew up affected me. I don't connect very well emotionally and I've been trying to work my way through that recently. It didn't matter before but it does now and I want to face my demons. Sorry, that sounds dramatic. I've realised that I don't want to be the sort of husband and father he was and I've been avoiding that possibility. I see it in Thomas sometimes, but it's not so bad and Ellie is a strong woman. She lets him know when he's out of line, he chose the right wife there. I've been afraid it goes down through the generations, I'm sure Dad had a hard upbringing."

"I don't think you're like your father," Sally assured him, "You're not even like Thomas. He's a good man but he's bull headed, you're much more sensitive and you think things through."

"I believe you now, I'm coming round to that," he said.

They arrived home and parted with an affectionate hug.

"It's been a lovely day, thank you," she said.

"Sorry to bend your ear on the way home," he was diffident now.

"No, I'm glad you told me, it's important to say these things."

She watched him walk over to the farm house to check in with Thomas; no-one ever returned to the farm without getting their finger back on the pulse of the day's events. She was at peace with her feelings for him now, there was a strong attraction but she understood that he had issues he needed to work through.

'He's not trying to mess me about,' she thought, 'I just need to get on with my own life now.'

Opening her laptop she found an email from Manchester inviting her for an interview which gave her something else to think about. Calling Marie to give her the news, she glossed over the details of her day with Josh; they had enjoyed themselves and made some good decisions about décor.

Marie's ewes were due to give birth in a couple of weeks and she was preparing the lambing shed. Thomas had offered to lend them some hurdles to make pens and Henry picked those up with the trailer.

"He says we can borrow a couple of heat lamps as well in case we have any weak lambs, but I didn't bring those over with the tractor in case I broke them."

"No worries," she replied, "I'll take the car over."

Arriving in the yard the first person she met was Josh. A good opportunity for a chat she thought, not sure if he knew Sally was thinking about moving away.

"I hear you and Sally had a successful trip to Exeter,"

she said.

"Yes, it was a nice day out and she helped me choose some lovely tiles. I think we're getting somewhere with the colour scheme now. She has such good taste, I reckon she could have a career as an interior designer."

"That might be more fun than the research job she's going for in Manchester."

He didn't know, she realised, seeing the stricken look on his face.

"When did this happen?"

"Oh, she's just heard she has an interview. On Tuesday I think."

"Is that what she really wants? To go back to life in the city?"

"I know she loves it on Exmoor but she hasn't anything to keep her here has she?"

There, she had thrown down the gauntlet. Josh ran a hand through his hair, standing in the farm yard he was having to think on his feet.

"Marie, you know how I feel about Sally."

"Well I can guess, but does Sally know? She's not a mind reader and I gather there have been some mixed messages though she doesn't tell me much."

"How do you think she feels?" he appealed to her, women were a mystery after all.

"I think she'd need convincing that you were serious and you want a proper relationship. But if you're asking me whether she's in love with you, yes, I think she is but she can't afford to admit it even to herself, she can't get hurt again."

"I would never hurt her," he said with conviction, "And I don't want to lose her."

"You'd better do something about it then," she told him, getting slightly exasperated, men were so slow on the uptake.

"She'll be back when, Wednesday?"

"Yes, someone from the Hall is meeting her off the train."

"Do you think you can get her to come to The Plough on Friday night then, we have a folk night and I'm playing."

"I expect I can twist her arm," this was getting interesting.

"Good, I do have some romance in my soul you know," he was smiling now. "I just need to let it out more."

"You and most of the men I know," she told him.

"Yeah, well, it's not very British is it? Let's get your lamps and I'll have a think. You won't say anything to her?"

"Of course not, that'd spoil it."

"You're a good friend to both of us Marie. I'm not going to mess this up."

Marie was smiling to herself as she drove out of the yard. 'I wonder what he'll come up with,' she wondered.

Sally came back from Manchester full of new impressions and was keen to share them with Marie.

"I don't know the city of course, but there are building sites everywhere, it's really booming. I stayed at a Premier Inn, cheap and cheerful. The company gave me the full tour, I was there four hours. I don't know if they invest that much time in all the candidates but I think I made a good impression. Funnily enough some of the research papers I have been translating relate to polymers in their field and that work has just been published so I wasn't giving away any trade secrets in talking about it. Of course they thought I was incredibly well informed, in fact they rather got the impression I had been involved with the German institute which produced it and of course I didn't comment."

"Do you really want this job then? Do you fancy city living again?"

'Poor Josh, have I made a mistake?' Marie wondered.

"Look, it's a good job with a reputable company and it's well paid, what more can I ask for? I don't really want to go back to the rat race if I'm honest and an over priced loft apartment is probably beyond me so I'd be looking to rent a flat outside the centre. It's back to commuting and I'd have to join the gym and try to make some friends.  But what's the point of renting a cottage somewhere on Exmoor and going on with the translating? It's a good way of contributing to a family income, flexible, you can do it from home, it's great for that, but as a whole way of life it's pretty lonely and soul destroying if I'm honest, and it doesn't progress to anything else."

"I take your point," Marie said evenly. "By the way, will you come down to The Plough with me on Friday night? They've got some music on and I feel like getting out before I have to get stuck into lambing."

"Why don't you go with Henry? The two of you could have a meal out, you might as well make use of my baby sitting services while you've still got me."

Marie was ready for that.

"Oh, Henry doesn't fancy it. He's got a lot of office work on this week and he wants a quiet start to the weekend. He's happy to look after the kids, and frankly, I fancy a girls' night out."

"Well, OK since you put it that way. Are you and Henry alright?"

This was so out of character.

"Yes, we're fine, really. I just thought it would be nice for us to go together especially if you're not going to be here forever."

"That's sweet of you," Sally was touched. " Will you pick me up then?"

"Yes, do you want to dress up a bit? Get in practice for city living?"

"You're a funny one, yes, why not? Nothing wrong with a bit of glamour."

Sally didn't know what had got into Marie, maybe she was playing some game trying to make Henry jealous. Perhaps he was getting a bit stuck in his ways.

When Marie knocked on the cottage door on Friday evening, Sally emerged wearing a fitted turquoise sheath dress which perfectly complemented her chestnut hair. Marie said,

"That's fabulous!"

"I'd like to say 'this old thing', but I picked it up in Manchester. Do you like it then?"

"It's just right, simple but elegant. How does it fasten, just a long zip at the back?"

"Well Duh! What do you expect, a row of Victorian buttons? Honestly, sometimes I think you're losing the plot lately," Sally was laughing.

"No, alright, it's convenient that's all, I thought it might be a side placket, they're so awkward to get off," Marie said airily.

"Are you thinking of taking up tailoring or something? And what happened to you dressing up then?"

"I put on clean jeans, that is dressing up for me these days."

"So, it's lucky I didn't over do it, I'd have stood out like a sore thumb."

Once in the car, Sally said ,

"I just got an email to say I got the job."

"Have you accepted it?" Marie was anxious.

"No, as I said, I just received it, they must have sent it last thing in the afternoon, I've got 'til Monday to reply."

"You don't sound very enthusiastic."

"It's started to come home to me that I'm leaving, but yes, I'm grateful they offered it to me. It's a good job."

When they arrived at the pub the acoustic night was just getting underway. A circle of musicians and singers was forming at one end of the bar and they waved to Josh who was seated against the far wall.

"I didn't realise he'd be here," Sally said. "I'll get the drinks, white wine?"

"Yes please, just a medium glass, I'm driving. I'll get us a seat."

Marie made for a table directly opposite Josh. That brought them to the edge of the circle, whereas she would normally sit further back, but there was no obligation to perform after all, and she wanted Sally to have a good view, whatever Josh was planning.

"I was looking for you over there," Sally said when she located their table but she sat down without complaint. The music was just beginning, a mixture of

207

traditional folk and more modern ballads, some people playing accordions or concertinas, or singing unaccompanied or with guitars. It was a friendly,lively crowd who all knew one another, with banter and applause and everyone joining in the choruses.

'I don't know if this is her sort of music,' Marie suddenly realised that she had no idea what Sally's taste was in music, what if she hated it? But then she realised that Sally was singing quite long choruses, she seemed to know all the words, that was a surprise.

Neither of them had heard Josh play before, but when he took up his guitar and his long fingers moved smoothly over the strings in the opening chords any doubts Marie might have had evaporated. Whatever he intended, Sally was bound to be impressed. He was looking straight across the circle at her as he sang Last Thing on My Mind. He was addressing her directly, though the others in the circle didn't notice, admitting he could have done better, he hadn't meant to hurt her, asking her not to go.

He sang well and there was more than polite applause.

Sally had got the message and he had her full attention. The music went on round the circle as they continued to exchange glances until the man next to Sally put down his accordion and the MC asked,

"Now, Ladies are you going to give us a song?"

Marie was about to tell him to pass them by when Sally said,

"I'll give you one."

There was a moment's expectant hush before she sang in a blues style which matched her rich expressive voice,

"Love, Oh Love, Oh Careless Love, you've wrecked the life of many a poor girl and you've surely wrecked this life of mine." A song redolent of disappointment and distrust, but tossed in Josh's direction with a tilt of her chin, it was more of a challenge.

Next time around he countered with a gentle song, "just want you to love me, I'm tired of sleeping alone." Her answer when her turn came was the traditional folk song One April Morning;
"Young men are false and full of deceiving, for they're roving and ranging, their minds are always changing..." She gave him an arch smile as she ended the song and he came over to offer them a drink.

"You're full of surprises," he wasn't deterred, putting his arm round her and giving her a squeeze before he went back to his seat. They had come to an understanding by now and they were both thoroughly enjoying the game.

"How come you know so many of these songs?" Marie asked.

"There was quite a folk scene when I was at uni in Glasgow," Sally told her. "Tell me, did you set this up?"

"No, Josh just asked me to get you here."

There was time for one more round of songs. Josh had spent hours in the last week choosing his final song and working out a guitar accompaniment. It was 'Lady,' which he had found in a Lionel Ritchie interpretation on You Tube. He sang passionately, telling her they were meant to be together, he wanted to wake beside her every morning, she was the love of his life.

By now the whole circle had cottoned on, so that everyone awaited Sally's response. So far she seemed to have rejected his heartfelt advances.

When it came to her turn, however she sang a setting of a Robbie Burns poem impenetrable to all but the folk fraternity who simply knew it as Ca' the Yowes, Call the Ewes ; the tale of a Highland lassie and her shepherd lover. Everyone joined in the chorus and she let Josh sing the fourth verse, "and in my arms you'll lie and sleep, and you shall be my dearie."

She sang the last verse to much applause, "If you'll stand to what you've said, I'll gang with ye my shepherd lad, and you may row me in your plaid and I shall be your dearie."

The evening was breaking up and Marie stood to leave.

"Are we going?" Sally asked.
"I am, unless you expressly don't want Josh to drive you home."
Decision time. Sally stood up and hugged Marie, "Thanks for everything," she said. "I hope your conniving was worth it."

"Let me know in the morning," Marie told her.

Marie looked back to see Josh weaving his way through the musicians packing up their instruments, guitar case in hand.

'Well, it's up to them now,' she thought.

Josh was very gallant, handing Sally into the car.

"What a fabulous evening," he said. "You look gorgeous, and you have a great voice, think of the duets we can do!" He reached for her hand.
"I love you Sally, please don't go to Manchester or anywhere else for that matter."

He stopped the car outside his house and leaned over

to kiss her.

"Come on," he said, pulling her out of the car, but then he hesitated.

"Are you coming in?" giving her the choice.

She raised her face to return the kiss and took his hand. Yes, she was coming in. He drew her straight towards the staircase, leading her up to his bedroom which she remembered as plain and austere. He opened the door, "wait there."

The room was in almost complete darkness although it was warm. She was aware of him crossing the floor and suddenly there was candle light reflected in the wardrobe mirrors and then more candles until the whole room was alight with a soft glow in which she saw red roses in glass jars. He came back to her, leading her into the room.

"I wasn't sure, but I hoped you would come."
The zip was indeed convenient and Sally unbuttoned his shirt. There was no fumbling haste and as their passion grew more urgent he led her to the bed where the freshly laundered linen smelled faintly sweet. Later, much later, they were lying in one another's arms.

" If I'd known you were going to sing that I'd have got a plaid to wrap you in," he teased her.

"There's a lot you don't know about me, Sir" she replied.

"Ditto I'm sure, but we have the rest of our lives to find out," and he kissed her, starting all over again.

They woke to early spring sunshine and for a moment just lay there, exchanging a loving look, savouring the moment. Suddenly Josh sat up.

"What's the time? Oh Hell, I'm supposed to be in the

yard, there are beasts to feed. I'm sorry Sweetheart, I have to go," heading for the bathroom.

Sally pulled on the first thing to hand, his shirt from last night.

"Tea or coffee?" she asked.

" A quick cup of tea then, thank you. What I really want is a leisurely cooked breakfast with you but that isn't going to happen."

"Tell you what, I'll bring you a toasted bacon and egg sandwich out to the yard, how's that?"

"I knew you were an angel the first time I saw you!"

Entering the cattle shed, Thomas was about to ask, "What time do you call this" or words to that effect when he saw his brother was kissing Sally and something in their attitude told him this wasn't the first time. The smell of the bacon sandwich made it quite a domestic scene. Back at the house he told Ellie but she was not surprised.

" I saw her crossing the yard a while ago in last night's dress, that's a dead giveaway."

Ellie was not best pleased at the prospect of Josh getting into a serious relationship; she had persuaded herself he was a natural loner and that her sons were going to inherit the farm.

Later in the morning Sally texted Marie; she would have quite liked to go over to share her news but the first lambs were being born so she had to be content with a phone call.

"I'm so pleased for you," Marie said, "And you don't have any doubts? You're doing the right thing turning down the job?"

"You've no idea, we're just so right for each other. I know it's going to be perfect."

Marie had never heard her sounding so excited and happy.

" Well I'm delighted for you. We'll catch up soon I promise."

# Chapter 14

Lambing at Holtbourne was very different from Handy Cross. They had not gone to the expense of scanning the ewes so they had no idea whether all were pregnant or how many singles or doubles to expect, so they brought the whole flock into the sheep shed and started to watch and wait.

The floor was covered in deep straw which they had to buy in, but that was more than paid for by selling the excess hay, and the sheep seemed more contented and calmer than the mass of ewes at Handy Cross which had milled about among others they did not recognise. Marie's small flock were bonded and they settled happily into the shed, which made for easier lambing when the time came. Most days at least two or three ewes went into labour and Marie was soon deprived of sleep since she was often in the shed all night. One evening she fell asleep in the straw and woke to find she was being nuzzled by a ewe who had newborn, healthy twin lambs at foot, luckily there had been no complications.

When things were quieter, Henry or Jack would go out in the evenings to check what was going on and George came over during the day, sending her back to the house to get some rest. Sitting in the straw with the lambs, he shared his experience and she learned a lot from him in his modest way. He arrived soon after one of her favourite sheep whom she called Doris gave birth to triplets, unusual but not unknown with sheep.

"She'll never feed all three," George told her, "so we need to see if we can palm the smallest off onto a ewe with a singleton. Now this one here that's just given birth isn't a first time mother, we might have a chance here. We need to rub the birth waters from her own lamb all over this one, you see, rub it well in, and hold the two lambs together so it really takes on the scent. Now, let's see if she'll take to it."

The two young lambs were returned to the ewe in her pen and both went over to suckle. The ewe didn't seem able to tell the difference and accepted both lambs as her own.

"There," said George with satisfaction. "You know you have to number each ewe and her lambs so you can pair them up again in the field if they get separated. I always do red for singles and blue for doubles. The lambs and ewes recognise each other's voices of course and in a small flock you aren't likely to get them separated, but young ewes can forget they've got two and so long as they have one with them they might not look for the other one. No ewe will allow another's lamb to suckle of course."

"At Handy Cross I saw them skin a dead lamb and tie the fleece to the back of an orphan so the ewe would think it was hers. That was a grizzly business."

"Yes, it does seem harsh but if you've got a ewe in milk with no lamb and a lamb without a mother it makes sense for both of them. Bottle fed lambs do alright but it's hard work, and they're always better off with a mother."

As it turned out all the ewes were pregnant and when

they had all lambed, George was taking stock.

"You've done well for your first season. That's a good tup, so you can use him again next year. You've ended up with more ewe lambs than ram lambs so they'll add to your flock; mind you, I don't know how many you want to keep in the end. I reckon the farm will support maybe sixty breeding ewes. Most of these bred doubles so you'll need a lot of grass through the summer but that shouldn't be a problem if we get the rain. Lambs have to make forty-five kilos to go to market."

To Marie the increase in numbers seemed a good return for her investment in the sheep but how much profit they would actually make remained to be seen.

George had arrived with what he called 'a nice brace of coneys.' Marie was making a casserole with the rabbits which George had skinned and paunched for her. He had got them in the pub from the owner of the ferrets and there was enough meat to save the saddle to make a pie. It was good country food and she was happy to eat them providing they had not come from their own farm.

'I know that's hypocritical but it's how I feel,' she thought and she knew the family would agree with her. She was bending down to put the dish in the oven when Henry came into the kitchen. Coming up behind her he nuzzled her neck and said,

"The kids are watching a movie, let's go upstairs." She turned to face him and returned his embrace but she objected,

" I probably still smell of sheep."

"Well, if you do, I've stopped noticing," he laughed, taking her hand and pulling her towards the stairs.

'No reason why Sally should have all the fun,' Marie thought, ' having kids doesn't need to be a passion killer.'

When at last she had a chance to catch up with Sally, Marie was curious.

"I gather it's all wonderful but what's going on?"

"I've moved in with Josh," Sally told her. "We've bought the basics, sofa, a couple of leather chairs, that sort of thing. Josh had a budget for that but it makes me angry when I think of all my good furniture being repossessed, still I have to let that go; I couldn't have taken it with me when I gave up the tenancy. Of course, he's a man so he already had an enormous TV. I've managed to contribute anyway, I paid for the curtains and towels, and some nice rugs."

"Have you given up the cottage then?"

"Yes, I was due to leave in a couple of weeks anyway. Ellie's being really odd though. I cleaned the place from top to bottom but she still sent the woman in who does the holiday lets, it was like she was taking possession of the place again. The cleaner basically got paid for two hours of doing nothing. Ellie definitely doesn't like me getting together with Josh; she warned me off before and I don't know if she just doesn't like being proved wrong, or she doesn't like me or what."

"She can be very judgemental, I've noticed that, maybe she doesn't approve of people living together."

"They don't go to church, I can't think it's that; she's friends with Carol and she has a partner, and Josh's Mum isn't married either. I think maybe she doesn't want another woman on the farm, that must be it; not that I interfere. I walk up with Josh to check the sheep, things

217

like that but that's all."

"Don't let her spoil it for you."

"No fear of that, Thomas is nice to me and he and Josh really get on. It's a jokey relationship but they're a partnership, I can't see him letting Ellie sour that."

"Well, you're good together, that's the main thing."

"Oh, I can't tell you, it sounds cheesy but it's true love. We miss each other if we're apart for a morning. In fact," she said laughing, " I'm going back  now to see if he can take a proper lunch break."

Marie hugged her, saying,

"I couldn't be happier for you."

'What a difference,' she thought as she waved her out of the door. 'She was fragile and brittle when she first came but she's blooming now. It shows what love can do.'

All winter Jack had been attuned to the season, sensing that the farm was sleeping, and the only sound he could detect was a low steady pulse in the landscape, like a subdued heart beat, but with Spring the music started again and grew in intensity. Sometimes he caught faint snatches of melody even during the day and at night from his window the strains were clearer.

As the moon waxed, his night binoculars revealed the creatures gathering in front of the Tump, and oddly, foxes and deer, rabbits and badgers stood or crouched motionless without fear of their natural predators, as if the laws of nature were suspended for a time. In the warm days as the grass grew and the trees came into leaf the animals and birds responded with a burst of activity.

Chloe came in from the stables saying,

" I've just seen a rabbit hopping away with a big wadge of hay in its mouth."

"She was lining her nest I expect," Marie said, "I wish I'd seen that though."

After school Jack would often sit on top of the Tump in the sunshine, or climb into the tree house. From those vantage points he saw a hare running across the upper pasture, a family of stoats in their brown summer coats playing along the hedge line and rabbits with their babies grazing in the orchard.

The dawn chorus was a cacophony of different notes, but the garden and meadow birds 6 sang all day long as they defended their territory and fetched food for their first brood of chicks and Jack was beginning to recognise the individual calls. It was not that he was studying the animals but rather that he let it all wash over him until he felt a deep connection with the landscape of which the living inhabitants formed only a part.

A lorry arrived with the two long poly tunnels Henry had ordered and in no time they were efficiently erected. He was grateful; thanks to Margaret, he had not had to attempt that job himself. As soon as the men left, he began setting up the staging and connecting hoses for the water supply; he couldn't wait to start growing. Marie came out to see what he was doing and was amazed at the size and height of the structures.

"It's all to increase air flow, it's going to be a complete eco system in here," he told her. "It seems like it's been a long time coming, but this is the bit of the whole enterprise I've been waiting for. This is what it's all about for me."

"I know it is, and when you have to be off the farm I'll make sure everything gets watered and looked after, you'll have to show me how."

"I'm relying on that," he replied. "If they dry out or get over-heated the crops will fail. And there need to be different areas. I'll have to learn where the warmer spots are for instance, so I can plant accordingly. I thought I would try some decorative plants which sell for high prices too, things like plumbago, oleander and hibiscus, and the sort of things people buy for their conservatories like clivias and stephanotis. I'll have to see what works."

Marie was glad to see him so enthusiastic and she had plans of her own. She called a meeting of craftspeople to have a look at the barn. Sophie and Hannah had been supportive from the start and they had been spreading the word, so there was plenty of interest as Marie explained how she saw it working. There was room for ten display stands and she would open from ten until four every day, handling the sales in return for a commission. They had set up a website, Instagram and Facebook page and she wanted to encourage everyone to blog about their work to promote the venue. She was printing flyers for the tourist information centres and asking accommodation providers to include them in their welcome packs.

"If anyone has any other ideas it would be great to have more input," she looked around to gauge the reaction and thought their investment in flooring and lighting was paying off, it was an attractive space and people were keen to be a part of it. She ended up with commitments from a variety of crafters including

Sophie's jewellery and Hannah's clothing of course, Judith's pottery, Jed's smaller metal work like fire-irons, weathervanes and candle holders, and a woman from the village who made jams and pickles.

The weekend before Easter she held a grand opening and invited the local press and radio station and even got an article published in the Exmoor Magazine.

As she looked around at the colourful display stands and local artwork on the walls Marie was impressed with the effect. Half the village had come, mainly out of curiosity but some were buying, and as Jack and Chloe handed out canapes and Henry and Josh, who had been roped in by Sally, served drinks, Marie was quietly confident.

"It all looks fabulous," Sally told her, giving her a hug. "You deserve this to be a real success. Listen, I've been thinking, I can come and sit in here for a few hours at a time. I can bring my laptop and if it's quiet I can get on with my work."

"That's really sweet of you and I'll ask if I'm desperate, but Hannah and Sophie are both going to do some shifts in return for reduced commission. It'll be a lot of effort to start with but if it takes off I can outsource the cooking and maybe pay for some help too."

Marie could see how it would all work out.

As the summer season got underway there weren't enough hours in the day for Marie; the sheep were out at pasture and the grass was growing well but she checked them over regularly and with the lambs there were far more to tend to these days. The hens were laying well and she had bought some Silkies and Bantams, cocks and hens to breed from since they were popular as pets.

They had to be kept in pens because they were just too vulnerable to the foxes; the vixen was often seen about the fields with her young cubs playing in the sunshine like puppies. On warm afternoons they were bold enough to lie about in a favourite spot, only moving on if the humans got particularly close.

Marie was baking cakes and scones but often had to let the family eat them or put them in the freezer, the craft gallery was not taking off as quickly as she had hoped. She set up her loom in the barn and got on with the weaving which was good in a way because she had not touched it for months, but she had rather be serving customers.

Tourists did wander in from time to time and they liked what they saw, most bought something and occasionally several items, but not enough people walked on past the church, that corner seemed to be a demarcation line and the publicity didn't seem to be getting the message across although the village was crowded.

Henry's vegetables grew well and regular egg customers and those tourists who did find their way to the gallery bought some but he had to sell the rest to the deli or the gastro pub at modest prices; they were not prepared to pay a premium for organic produce.

Henry told Marie,

"I've really got to do a site visit to Masons. I can't just leave it to Adam and Jason all the time, there are things I have to see for myself and next week I'll have to spend a few days in the office. You will keep a good eye on the watering won't you, and keep the ventilation going?"

"Yes, of course, " she assured him. "I've done it

before, I won't forget."

"I know, but now it's heating up things dry out quickly and if you don't open the doors both ends before midday it's like a furnace in there."

She promised to bear that in mind.

As it happened, the day Henry left was the beginning of a heat wave and Marie was especially busy. A group of tourists spent an hour in the gallery, drinking tea and eating cake, talking about the village, and Marie was pleased when they each bought several items.

This was more like it, if only this happened every day. By the time they went she thought she should check the sheep and give the hens some more water. It was not until the children were home from school and she was giving them their tea that she suddenly remembered the poly tunnels. She ran outside praying,

'He only went this morning, surely it will be alright.'

The doors were still firmly closed and when she opened them a blast of scorching hot air came out. Under the plastic covering the temperature was well over thirty degrees and the foliage had all collapsed; it looked like a total disaster. She ran around opening all the doors and watering the plants.

'What am I going to tell Henry?' she thought.

Her first instinct was to call him and confess what she had done but she knew there was no advice he could give her to retrieve the situation and he couldn't come rushing back, it would only worry him. She went back out every half hour and as the evening cooled the temperature came down until at last she felt she had to close the doors in case the now saturated plants got chilled.

When Henry called her in the evening she said nothing about it, although he said,

"You sound a bit down, has anything happened?"

"I've just had a busy day that's all," she tried to sound brighter, and told him about the encouraging sales she had made.

At last going back into the tunnels by torchlight towards midnight, she thought the plants were beginning to revive a little and by morning, to her surprise they seemed to have recovered. Over the next couple of days she watched them anxiously in case the flowers or fruits dropped but apart from a couple of shrivelled leaves which she removed guiltily from the base of some of the stems, she seemed to have been lucky.

When Henry got back he went out to see his precious plants and she held her breath until he returned.

"Has everything been alright then?" he asked casually.

She felt she had to say something so she answered,

" Actually, I was surprised how quickly they do dry out and it does get very hot in there doesn't it? I might have been a bit late opening the doors."

"You've been in there often enough with me, you know you have to check on them regularly. The one thing I ask you to do while I'm gone..."

If he was upset now, thank Heavens he hadn't seen them at their worst, she thought.

In fact Henry had been having a difficult time while he was away. He had made the site visit to Mason's and found the younger men had missed something important in the accounting system which put a different perspective on his view of the business. He was going to have to re-evaluate some of the comments he had already put in a preliminary report which had gone to the partners. Back at the office, he had back pedalled as far as he could, but the discrepancy was going to be obvious and he expected one or other of the partners to pick up on it. The truth was, he should be doing many more of the site visits himself instead of delegating them to Jason and Adam.

# Chapter 15

Over at Handy Cross, Josh wished he could make some adjustments to his work life balance too.

"Honestly, I'm not complaining," Sally told him, "But you do seem to work all hours without any proper time off."

"I'm sorry, Sweetheart, but there's always something on a farm, no sooner do we get through calving than it's hay harvest, we have to keep on top of pests in the crops and then it's the cereal harvest. It's dawn to dusk in the summer, but I will try to get the evenings off at the weekends unless we're up against it and the weather is about to break."

She had to be content with that. Under other circumstances she would have asked Ellie how she found it, but they weren't on very friendly terms these days; anything Ellie said always seemed to have a sting in the tail.

They had a Barbecue for Ryan's birthday and there were enough people to dilute the atmosphere a bit, but Ellie avoided coming over to chat to Sally. The Freemans were invited and Marie admitted later to Sally that she saw the problem. She was getting some meat from the grill where Thomas was cooking when Ellie said,

"Josh hasn't done a thing to help you all evening."

"Oh, he's OK," Thomas replied smiling, "He seems to have his hands full."

They were looking over to where Josh was seated on an old teak chair with Sally on his knee.

"He helped set up, and I'm doing just fine. Here you go Marie."

She carried the food back to Henry and the children, sitting on some straw bales under a tree.

"What a perfect evening," he said, stretching. " If it could always be like, this life would be wonderful."

"I know we're busy, but isn't this what we wanted?"

"Yes, of course it is, but I hate having work things nagging away in the background. And now I've mentioned it, there it is again."

"I'm sorry you feel that way, I wish you didn't have to do it. Maybe by next summer we'll be making a proper living; we knew this year would be tough, we've only  had the farm twelve months."

"You know what's sad?" he said, "We forgot the date and were too busy to celebrate the anniversary of moving in."

"You're right. Well, let's raise a glass to it now and try to relax in the here and now, look at those stars coming out. We live here, we're not on holiday, we own a farm on Exmoor, now that is worth celebrating isn't it?"

"You're right, I'm sorry to be grouchy. What are the kids doing?"

"They're over there on the rope swing."

"Oh yes, they love it, don't they? We did the right thing bringing them here."

"Of course we did." She wondered what had got into Henry, it wasn't like him to be pessimistic.

Sally and Josh came over and the women were soon

sitting under the tree discussing Ellie's attitude.

"I swear she's getting worse," Sally said.

"Do you think the weather will hold?" Henry asked Josh. "I want to make our hay this week; I would have done it before but I had to go away for work."

"You should be alright, it's set fair for a few days. We've got ours in already."

"Yes, I noticed as we came up."

"Listen, I can give you a hand. If you cut and turn it I'll bring our small tractor over and bale with you and help you haul it. You want small bales, right?"

"Yes, but I can't ask you to do that, Thomas won't be pleased if you're off the farm."

"Well he doesn't own me."

"I have to say it would be great if you can spare the time. Poor old George was pretty exhausted at the end of it last season and he's another year older now."

"No worries, we can do it in a day. I owe Marie a favour. If it wasn't for her, Sally would be in Manchester and I'd be here on my tod and I wouldn't be a happy boy. Ellie has persuaded Thomas to take the boys to Centre Parks for a few days before school starts and I'll be holding the fort then, so he can't complain."

"Are you thinking of taking a holiday yourselves this year?" Henry had gathered from Marie that Sally felt they were not getting enough quality time.

"Not immediately, but I think when we do go it'll be the big one."

"Oh, are congratulations in order then?"

"I haven't asked her, but I know what I want. I don't mean to rush her though and anyway, I can hardly get down on one knee in the cow shed."

228

" No, but my advice as an old married man is not to hang about too long. I've learned that women do like the grand gesture, they like to feel appreciated."

"Thanks mate, I'll bear that in mind."

Marie stood up and shook the clinging straw off her skirt.

"Time to go I think." She kissed Sally and hugged Josh. "I'll just thank  Ellie and Thomas and say goodbye to the birthday boy. Henry can you round up the kids?"

They made their way back to the car; the kids were running ahead and Henry put his arm round Marie.

"I'm sorry if I seem  negative darling, I'm just a bit down about work."

"You can tell me about it tomorrow, you know I want to share anything that's bothering you."

"What would I do without you?" he said, kissing her hair, but he wasn't going to worry her with his anxiety.

Henry got a summons to go up to the office and put it off until the hay was in; the farm was his priority now. Driving up the motorway he steeled himself for a confrontation, a dressing down at the least. It was inevitable that he would make a mistake at this distance. He had misjudged Adam and Jason's competence and failed to supervise them properly; it would look as if he was slacking and in this industry that wouldn't go unnoticed.

With these gloomy thoughts he went up in the lift and presented himself in the partner's office. Now it was Mr. Gropey who did not mince words.

"I have had to waste valuable time evaluating the

229

work you have done on the Mason contract and I think you will not be surprised when I say it's slap dash and not what we expect from someone of your calibre. Apart from the obvious error which you noticed almost too late to correct, and that has involved a delay while you amended your report, the project should be almost finished by now and you are way behind. I have spoken at length with Adam and Jason and I am not apportioning blame to them ; they were out of their depth and you left them to it. I'm not sure what you're playing at Henry, maybe the country air has gone to your head but it's just not good enough.

When you moved away last year we cut you some slack; you had done the basic work on that project before you went and it took longer than it should to wrap it up. This year, we gave you a small simple contract to handle, frankly below your pay grade, and you have clearly not given it your full attention.

Look Henry, you've been with us some years now and we know what you're capable of producing. We don't want to lose you, but this is crunch time. Either you come back into the office full time in line with your terms of employment or we're going to have to let you go. Frankly, I don't see the problem man, if you want to keep this country house then get accommodation in town during the week, or you've got family to stay with haven't you? No problem then. I have to say we'd want to see some real commitment from now on but we're prepared to overlook this aberration. I think that's very generous don't you?"

Henry took a deep breath. He had sensed this was coming, all he had been doing was buying himself time, but he knew it wasn't enough. The farm wasn't nearly ready to support them, if it ever would be. He pushed that knowledge to the back of his mind and set about maintaining his dignity.

"I appreciate your offer, and yes, it is very generous in the circumstances, but I can't spend all week here, I need to work from home."

There was a moment's silence while the man across the desk took that in.

"So you're refusing to work from the office?" He raised his eyebrows in disbelief. "Is there some situation at home your wife can't cope with? Is anyone ill?"

Maybe he had a kid with leukaemia or Mary or whatever she was called had mental health problems. He couldn't imagine anyone in their right mind throwing up a job like this.

"No, it's nothing like that, but there's no point in living on Exmoor if you can't actually be there."

"You've lost me I'm afraid, unless you've won the lottery of course. Have you had some extraordinary stroke of good luck?"

"I only wish I had. I'll be honest, I really do need this job but I can't spend all week in the office."

"Well," his boss said, standing up to conclude the interview, "Maybe there's some small consultancy I've never heard of in Exeter or somewhere which will be glad of your services, and I would give you a good reference, but it doesn't look as if you have a future with us. Take the weekend to think about it and talk it over with your wife, she may have a very different view. Let me know what you decide on Monday."

He offered his hand and Henry shook it and left the

office in a daze of euphoric relief tinged with panic. He was free and immediately he couldn't wait to be back on the farm, but the consequences of what he had just allowed to happen settled like a black cloud in his mind. They depended on his salary to pay the mortgage and much more and he had just thrown all that to the winds.

Back at his parents' house he packed his bag in a hurry. Luckily his father was playing golf so he avoided that scrutiny for the moment, he wasn't even going to imagine what his reaction would be.

"You're back early dear," his mother said. "There's some ham in the fridge if you want a sandwich. It's my bridge afternoon so I must shoot off."

She kissed his cheek and left in a hurry, typically oblivious to his agitated state. On this occasion he could only be grateful for her self absorbed obtuseness. He did make himself a sandwich, feeling in need of something solid in his stomach and then, almost overcome by a sudden weariness, climbed back into the car to head for home. Now his dominant thought was,

'How am I going to tell Marie?'

It was early evening by the time he passed the impressive facade of the National Trust property, lit by mellow sunshine in the last heat of the day. He turned into the High Street where tourists still drifted in search of dinner and a drink and wound his way down the lane, narrowed by a mass of rose bay willow herb and cow parsley to his own beloved farm.

It was always such a pleasure approaching home, first recognising the familiar landmarks as he left the main road, driving through the village until at last he turned in at the gates into the green oasis of his own domain. This evening it was all especially poignant, a dagger to the heart.

'I can't be the cause of us losing all this,' he thought.

As usual, Marie came to kiss him and the children crowded round, telling him what they had done in his absence.

"Some lambs got out and we had to catch them."

"Josh brought his dog over and he ran off with Taffy."

He looked to Marie for an explanation and she shrugged saying,

"I hadn't noticed she was in season. Merle is a nice looking collie and a good working dog, if she has puppies they may even be worth something."

He didn't know whether to be pleased or not, another complication maybe or a small contribution to the pot? Either way it wasn't going to make much difference in the scheme of things.

"You look tired," Marie said. "Go and sit down and I'll bring you a beer."

"I'd better just check the tunnels first."

"Of course, but it's all fine out there." She'd learned her lesson the last time.

It was not until the children had gone up to bed that Henry said,

"Sit down, I'm afraid we really have to talk."

Looking at his face she could tell whatever was worrying him had come to a head. When he had told her everything, he sat with his head in his hands, wishing he could have kept this news from her. Marie listened with growing dismay but she also had a small voice in her head saying,

'You knew this would happen, he couldn't concentrate on both, you saw things were slipping.'

Why hadn't she warned him not to just plod on doing the minimum? The answer was that she recognised his heart was no longer in it and from the start she had doubts that he could keep the job going, she had just hoped it would last longer than this.

She looked at him sitting there, looking defeated, his shoulders slumped and her heart went out to him.

"This isn't your fault darling," she said with conviction. "Look at me."

He did look up and drew from her strength and resolve.

"This was bound to happen, you've done well to keep it going this long. When we bought the farm there was a lot we didn't take into account and it's taking longer than we ever thought to make it work but on so many levels it's right for us and we won't give up now. We're going to make a living somehow without you selling your soul to do it. It's late and you're exhausted. Let's go to bed and try to get some sleep. We'll look at the figures tomorrow and see how we can budget, but you know we're in this together whatever happens. We're a good team and we went into this with our eyes open. We'll manage somehow, we always do."

She had no idea how they were to make a living now, but she had to carry the family for a while until Henry recovered his self belief.

# Chapter 16

It was afternoon the next day before Henry and Marie gathered their paperwork together and sat down in the sitting room to look at their finances. Chloe was out riding with Tamsin and Lucinda, and Jack was out in the woods with his mountain biking friends. They made a long list of their outgoings, everything from the mortgage and council tax down to animal feed. It made a daunting total. Offset against that was the relatively pathetic sum raised by egg and vegetable sales and the small commission from the gallery together with the ponies' livery.

"We'll be sending some of the lambs to market and we can sell some hay again but that's about it," Henry said wearily. "Frankly even with increased production from the poly tunnels and the sale of a few ornamental chickens, even if the gallery did a bit better next year it doesn't amount to a viable income and we've got a long winter to get through first."

Marie couldn't argue with the facts.

"So what do you think?" she asked with a sinking heart.

Neither of them noticed Jack hovering in the doorway. He withdrew into the hall but sat down on the bottom stair to listen.

"I know this is our dream and I can't bear to think of giving it up so soon, but I can't see a way forward. We've invested a great deal, more than we could afford, in getting the place up and running and we aren't quite in the red yet but we've used up the contingency fund as you well know."

She nodded dumbly, fighting down the misery that threatened to choke her. She knew what he was going to say next.

"There's no doubt we've added value to the place, we haven't renovated the house to some people's standards but we've done a lot and the buildings are in good repair now, anyone looking at it would see the potential. We couldn't sell it as a business as it is, but anyone with money could convert the gallery into holiday units and maybe the machine shed and some of the other stone buildings as well."

"Couldn't we do that?" she asked. "I'd hate to have people here all the time but it'd be better than having to leave."

"I've thought of that but we couldn't service that kind of loan as well as the mortgage, even if someone would lend us the money. It'd be a huge investment."

She nodded and swallowed hard.

"So what do you think we should do?"

"Practically? We should put it back on the market using the internet this time of course and whatever profit we make can go towards a smaller mortgage on a better house than we had before, because I'm damned if I'm going back where we came from with my tail between my legs, though I expect a lot of people would see this as a wise temporary investment. We could live in a village outside Exeter and go back to working for other people. You have your background in education and my skills are transferable even if there isn't a management consultancy to apply to."

"Is that what you want?" she asked.

"What I want? No, I'd hate it but we may have no choice."

"Actually," she said, "I can't see us doing it,we might just have become temperamentally unemployable."

"Well, we don't have to decide now." Henry sighed, " If we don't put the farm on the market now we can go through another winter, but I warn you, we'll inevitably start racking up debt and that goes against the grain for both of us. I'm not sure how much we'd enjoy living here either, feeling we were just postponing the inevitable. Anyway my love, it's all a lot to take in, we don't have to decide immediately, but I'm afraid the writing is on the wall."

"I'll make a cup of tea," she said, standing up, "And then I'd better check the sheep."

Jack slipped through the kitchen and ran across the yard, not stopping until he reached the Tump. There he slumped down at the base of the hillock, his back against the vertical side which was covered with ivy and the tough thick fibrous stems left by decades of wild clematis, the 'old man's beard.'

He sat motionless watching the hare and her leverets grazing, her long muscular body bearing little resemblance to a rabbit, her long ears twitching to detect any unusual sound, the powerful legs bunched ready for the characteristic jinking sprint from danger.

Jack's mind was blank, his spirit sunk in deep despair when he became aware of a warm furry nose poking itself up towards his face and Taffy's wet tongue licking the tears he had not been aware he was crying. He got up crossly thinking, 'Here I am blubbing like a girl,' and ran round to climb the steep side of the Tump, arriving breathless on the top where he cried out in anguish,

"No, you can't let this happen. I won't leave here!" though he didn't know whom he was addressing.

He sat on the top of the mound with Taffy at his feet, feeling churlish and angry, ranging over ridiculous solutions in his mind. Taffy got bored and started to sniff about and then, seeing a lizard basking in the sun on the rocky edge she started to scrabble, although the lizard had long since slipped away. Annoyed by the sound of her claws against the rock, Jack got up, saying,

"What are you doing you daft dog?" and came over to make her stop.

It was then that he saw what the dog had uncovered, a smooth plate of dark rock which extended up from the base to the top of the Tump. Jack drew back the ropes of clematis and saw that there were some kind of regular marks on the rock, making a line like a curved  picture frame. Yes, there was definitely carving on the rock face. He lay down and leaned over as far as he could to reveal more and saw further lines leading downwards. He scrambled back to the bottom of the Tump and started frantically to pull away at the ivy and clematis ropes which clung tenaciously to the face of the rock.

At last he had seen enough to convince him that he was uncovering a figure, there were the legs, the cloven hooves on pointed feet. He sank to his knees in front of it and took time to reflect. Shall I tell them about this or cover it over again? It came to him that this had been revealed precisely when he had cried out in desperation for help. He couldn't see how it would solve the financial problems, but releasing the power in the landscape could only lend force to his determination not to leave. He was melded to this land and had called on it for aid, and this surely was the response.

Suddenly quite calm, Jack went into the house to find his parents.

They were in the kitchen preparing a meal and he could see the strain on their faces.

"I've found something you've got to see," he told them. "Come and look."

Something about his quiet insistence made them follow him back to the Tump.

"You see?"

They did see and it was a revelation to them both because neither of them had paid much attention to the half heard stories about past goings on at Mennad Hall or the healing power in the spring or whatever Sally might have said about a portal in the landscape.

Nevertheless by the following morning they had cleared the face of the Tump and what was revealed in the rock was extraordinary by any reckoning. Whether the plate of black rock was a natural feature which had been smoothed to form a plaque or had been sunk into the face of the hillock at some time was unclear but there was unmistakeably a figure etched deep into it, even framed by an arching line forming a rounded doorway such as you find in a very old church.

"It looks like a, what d'you call it, a satyr," Marie said. "Does this have something to do with the Hall ? Sally was telling me about that but I didn't take it all in, I'll give her a call."

"Wait a minute," said Henry, "I don't think we should just start telling everyone about this until we know more about it and have decided what we want to do."

"How do you mean?"

"This could be a significant find and we don't want a media scrum before we've taken stock. It's on our property and we don't want hordes of druids or something descending on us, or even archaeologists."

"I want to show it to Dr. Laidlaw," Jack said, "But not anyone else for the moment."

"OK, good thinking, she wrote a book about local folklore didn't she? Maybe she knows about it," said Marie.

Jack went up to the caravan and knocked on the door.

"Hello young Jack, you look like a man with a mission, what can I do for you?"

"We've found a carving in the rock on the Tump and we want you to look at it."

"Have you indeed? That's very interesting, let me get my coat."

Lilian Laidlaw stood back and assessed their find. Marie was impatient for her verdict.

"Jack thinks it might be the Greek god Pan, but I wondered if it was a satyr."

"It's neither of those," Lilian was decisive. " Pan is always depicted as having pipes and this figure appears to carry a horn, and he is wearing a torque around his neck. Anyway his antlers rule out either of those possibilities; a satyr has small goat horns . If it were either of those it would argue for this being carved in Gerard Sinclair's time, part of his Dionysian fantasy world, but if he knew about this his rites would have been very different. This is the real thing, a much older deity. There was a small revival of his cult in Victorian times as the god of the witches, we humans subvert and misappropriate everything don't we? But that wouldn't account for a carving on Exmoor."

" I know who he is," said Jack, "But what's his name?"

"Yes," said Lilian. "You may know him better than anyone and he has been called various names, but in ancient Gaul he was known as Cernunnos, the horned god, Lord of the Wilds. It's not surprising if he was known to the peoples of Western Britain, though we have to wonder why his image was carved here in this remote spot. It may be connected with the healing spring of course, and that argues for this being a site of importance in ancient times, perhaps a place of gathering for worship."

Marie shivered, this other worldly stuff was a bit disconcerting and she needed a bit of normality.

"Let's go in and have a cup of tea," Marie suggested.

Settled in the kitchen, she asked,

"So, Gerard Sinclair wasn't wrong when he thought there was a sort of portal here? Sally said you mentioned that."

"It's true that he founded his cult here because he thought it was a source of power; I don't know if he sensed that for himself or someone introduced him to it. But I suppose he thought in terms of Greek mythology because, like all public school boys, he had a classical education," Lilian said.

"We were drawn here too, it seems," said Henry.

241

" The whole of Exmoor has that effect to some extent of course, you come for a weekend and want to stay for life. But the pull is even stronger here, it's like a magnet."

"Exactly, perhaps lay lines intersect here, that would be worth looking into."

"I think Cernunnos, or whatever he is called, is more connected to animals than human beings," said Jack. "He's a guardian, like a shepherd, and when he calls they come. The funny thing is, at those times they forget to be afraid of each other and the foxes don't try to catch the rabbits."

"He is said to be a peacemaker among the animals; if you've seen that it's a confirmation," Lilian nodded.

Henry and Marie exchanged glances, feeling out of their depth in this conversation. The more they looked at their son, the more they saw a resemblance to the face in the rock; perhaps it was Jack who was meant to come here, or was he being taken over by something? Marie shivered.

Henry turned to the more practical aspects of their discovery.

"So what should we do, publicise it and let in anyone who wants to visit ? We don't want hordes of people tramping over the farm and I'm not sure even though it's been revealed now, that was the intention. It doesn't sound as if any historian would know more than Dr. Laidlaw, but could an expert be sure when the carving was done?"

"I doubt if you will get a definitive answer," Lilian replied, " And as to its meaning or intention, I think you have to decide how you want it to be seen, don't let anyone else dictate that."

"We can't hide it for long; George drops in, the crafters are around and tourists come to the gallery. Any one of them could notice," Marie said.

"You're right, we don't have long. We need to decide what to do about it, but first we need to understand what it means, and Jack, you should please tell us what has been going on with you. You've never mentioned any of this and we're concerned, you know? Dr. laidlaw seems to know more than we do."

Henry turned to Lilian for an explanation.

"Living as close to nature as I do," she replied, "You notice things in the silence and tune in to the landscape and its inhabitants. For some time I have been hearing notes of music drifting up from this farm but not the sort of thing you get from someone's radio. It is carried on the air on particular nights. I knew no more about it than that, except when Jack made a chance remark I realised that he heard it too."

"And you Jack," Henry turned to his son. "What can you tell us?"

"As soon as we moved in I started hearing the music coming from the Tump at night, not all the time but if the moon is full it's louder, and the animals come and stand around as if they are listening too. There's a figure that looks like solid mist that sits on the top of the Tump but I can't see him clearly. This summer the feeling is getting stronger as if the whole farm is throbbing and something is going to happen. I asked for help because I heard you talking about selling the farm and I just couldn't bear to leave here, and then immediately I found the carving. I think we're meant to use it to stay here but I don't think

243

it's shown itself just for that, it's as if it's the right time for it to be found."

Marie said,

"Actually, I would like Sally's input, she does Tarot readings and she's very intuitive."

"The girl from the library?" Lilian asked. "She's a good researcher I do know that."

Lilian felt she had revealed more than she intended during that encounter.

Sally brought Josh over with her, which wasn't quite what they expected, but when they came in after examining the carving, they both had thoughtful contributions to offer. Marie rustled up sandwiches and cake; this was turning into a brain storming session and the enlarged group gathered round the kitchen table again.

"I'm getting the impression from what Lilian says about the horned god, the Lord of the Wilds, that he isn't like the Green Man, John Barleycorn, who is sacrificed like the corn that has to die in the ground to multiply and grow again in the Spring. He's a guardian of the landscape and animals, am I right?" Sally looked round for agreement. "If the earth is a mother, then he is a father figure, a co-creator if you like. The female principle is the womb, the earth itself and the springs of water which flow from it are always an expression of the feminine force of course. But here is something new; if Gaia or whatever we call her gives birth to creation and gives form to the animals and all the life upon the earth, then the active male principle energizes and preserves it. It's a force for harmony and right living."

"There isn't a lot of that going on in the modern

world," Henry said with feeling.

"Not in commerce and industry maybe, or even in big agribusiness," said Josh, "But we farmers have always tended animals and preserved the countryside, otherwise it would be just forest and peat bog. We can live in harmony with nature and still live off the land."

"Are we agreed then that this discovery in our own times is a reminder of a more sustainable way of living, less exploitation," said Henry, "And if it does hold a message, we should publicise it in a controlled way."

"I'm afraid the first thing you have to do is chain up the side gate off the bridle path and keep your main gates closed or you'll have people camping in front of the Tump chanting and playing drums," said Josh.

"What a ghastly thought," Lilian shuddered. Jack was horrified.

"Don't worry," said Henry. "We'll plan this very carefully. Let's sleep on it and share any thoughts tomorrow. I want to thank Lilian and you two for your input, we've got some understanding of this now."

Lilian made her way back up the path to the hill but Josh said,

" D'you mind if we just have another look at the carving before we go?"

The golden glow of early evening  highlighted the rock as Sally and Josh were once more engrossed in the powerful image.

"It's quite something isn't it?"

Sally turned to Josh. His answering kiss was long and warm and for a few precious minutes she rested in his embrace before the carving, her head on his shoulder with a feeling of security and peace which was new in her life. They stood wrapped in a shared sense of joy and gratitude until he drew back to look at her face and said,

"I want this to last forever, will you marry me Sally?"

"Oh yes," she answered without hesitation.

As dusk fell and the Tump was deserted at last, the fox family came out and a few hinds jumped nimbly over the fence from the wood. It didn't take long for nature to reclaim her territory once the humans had gone.

Henry and Marie sat down after supper with the children to discuss their options. Obviously Jack had to be consulted at every stage, it was unthinkable to do anything he wasn't happy with, but Chloe could not be left out either. She didn't understand all the implications but she liked the idea of having a tea room and making the most of the gallery ; she was sociable and liked chatting to the tourists.

At nine and eleven the children would soon enough have the choice of becoming involved in any business they developed to support the farm. All idea of selling up had now been shelved.

"We can sell bottled water again, that's been done before here and  we don't need to make any actual claims about the spring having healing powers," Marie said.

"We need to print a pamphlet about the carving to explain what it is and its significance," Henry suggested.

Their minds were so full of ideas that they didn't sleep well that night but that didn't matter, the relief at finding a way forward was refreshing in itself.

George came up in the morning and was astonished at their discovery.

"You mean it's been there all this time, hidden under the old man's beard and we never knew? Well this'll cause a stir and no mistake. If you're not careful, you'll have every Tom, Dick and Harry wandering all over the farm."

"We're going to have to fence off a path from the yard up to the Tump," said Henry.

George was eager to help.

"That's easy enough, we can nick a bit of land from these two fields and move the fence over. I'll give you a hand with that later, we can do a rough job for now and maybe some proper post and rail later."

"That's good of you George, and I'll leave it to you to tell the village if you like," Henry knew how much George would relish that down at The Plough, it would make him quite a local celebrity by association.

Out of courtesy, they despatched Sally up to the Hall to invite Anthony to view the carving. He came round with her and accepted a cup of coffee, as amazed as everyone else at what they had uncovered.

"I must say, my father dismissed Gerard's activities as a narcissistic personality cult centred on himself, an excuse to surround himself with gullible young society women and indulge in a fantasy of his own devising. I have to conclude this casts rather a different light on his motives, although I don't think he had any real grasp of what he was dealing with. I'm glad it is you who have made this discovery and it didn't happen while I owned the farm. I don't envy you all the attention this will attract and I'll thank you to keep me and the Hall well out of it."

"Don't worry," Henry assured him. "Any reference to

the Hall will be kept well in the past, there's no reason why anyone should be interested in going there now."

"Nevertheless, I will instruct everyone to keep an eye out for intruders. I don't suppose you could just keep all this under wraps, cover it up again and forget all about it? No, I see that's unrealistic. Well, I hope no harm will come of it that's all."

On this pessimistic note Anthony left them to it and showed no further interest in the carving.

News of their discovery spread outwards like rings when a stone is thrown into a pond. First people came from the village to see what had been concealed for so long on their doorstep, then visitors from further across the moor and an increasing stream of tourists who heard about it while they were on holiday and that led to a steady growth in sales at the gallery and a demand for cream teas and ploughman's lunches.

# Chapter 17

The fenced path kept people from straying over the farm and on the whole any disruption could be contained. The phone began to ring with enquiries from further afield and it fell to Henry to deal with them. Local radio and TV wanted to come over for interviews; he put them off for a day to give themselves a chance to tell their families the news before they heard some other way.

Marie phoned her mother who was pleased and excited.

" Can we come down and see it?  Will we be in the way since you're so busy?"

Marie knew that on the contrary her parents would muck in and help.

"No Mum, do come, you were planning a visit before the end of the holidays anyway weren't you? We'd love to see you. Things are changing here, you know Jack will be going on the bus to senior school in a few weeks, that'll make for some early starts. I'm not sure I'm looking forward to that."

Henry decided to call Margaret before telling his parents, since she had been so encouraging about the poly tunnels. He sent her a picture of the carving on What's App and then phoned.

"I can't believe what I'm seeing," she said, "And it's really that big? It's not an illusion in the photograph?"

"It's virtually the height of the Tump," he assured her.

"Well that'll do you some good I imagine, it must be

attracting a lot of attention."

"We've hardly begun yet, but it's already improving sales in the gallery and I'm selling more produce direct."

"You might be overwhelmed, initially at least."

"If it gets too manic, we can get people to book visitor slots online."

"I don't know how you're going to fit it all in with working as well."

"Ah well, I've had to give up the day job."

"Oh I see. Isn't that a bit precipitate?"

"To be honest, it was on the cards anyway, I couldn't give it my best at a distance and it was starting to show. This is looking like a bit of a life saver in fact."

"Dad will have a field day saying 'I told you so,' but now you can make a success of this and prove him wrong. I'm glad for you little brother, it looks like you got a lucky break."

" And how are things with you?"

"Since you ask, I'm in line to be made a QC but it's under wraps at the moment so don't tell anyone."

"Really, that's great, you've worked for it Heaven knows. And what about your friend with the Italian connection?"

"Oh, that's on hold, for the moment at least, a bit of a silly slip up really," Margaret was putting a brave face on it.

"I'm sorry,Sis, I'm sure it wasn't just a casual fling to you, well for either of you really. I was wondering just how blind his wife could be though."

"I know, but I've lots to get on with. I don't suppose I'll get down before the end of the year but I'll look out for your find to hit the news headlines."

"You know you're welcome anytime Maggs, just turn up if you get a few days."

"Maybe I'll try for a long weekend then, it'd be good to see you."

Once again, he was left feeling sorry for his successful sister.


Henry was not looking forward to telling his parents; whatever he shared with them it always ended on a sour note. It was his mother who answered the phone and he attempted to describe the Cernunnos to her.

"What a strange thing to find buried on the farm, will it be treasure trove? Do you have to hand it over to a museum?"

"No Mum, it's on our land so it's ours."

"Still, it's on some sort of a plaque you say, I expect you'll get something for it at auction. If it's an antique, do you think Christie's would be interested?"

"No Mum, it's part of the landscape, part of the farm."

This was hopeless. He felt like leaving it there, but he might as well get it over with.

"Is Dad there?"

"He's just watching the news, I'll see if he wants to talk to you."

After a while his father came on the line.

"Ah, I'm glad you've phoned, you haven't told us when you're next due into the office. Your mother and I want to go away for a few days with the Hendersons so we need to know."

His parents would never entrust him with a key and let him use the house on his own. Did they think he would hold drunken parties or set the place on fire? Anyway, that was irrelevant now.

"I won't need to stay again Dad, I've given up the job."

He held the phone away from his ear, anticipating the explosion. He didn't have long to wait.

"You've done what? Have you completely lost your senses? How do you imagine you're going to make a living now? Not from that run down small holding I'm sure of that."

What if his father worked himself up to a stroke? Would he feel guilty? Yes, probably he would. Thank God he had something to distract his father from the loss of his job; supposing he was forced to have this conversation and they hadn't discovered the carving. It didn't bear thinking about. He let his father rant on until he ran out of steam.

" I have something to tell you Dad. We've found an ancient rock carving on the farm and it's going to attract a lot of attention on the media, so I thought I'd tell you in advance. You don't want to have to admit ignorance if the Hendersons mention it do you?"

"Why on earth would the Hendersons be interested in anything that goes on down there? I really do think you've lost the plot Henry, you're becoming very small minded and parochial. I don't know what to tell our friends when they ask how you're doing, it's embarrassing frankly. I can't imagine what Margaret will make of you throwing up your career, she's going up in the world, unlike you."

"I know Dad, we've  had a long chat and I 'm very pleased for her," Henry said wearily. "I'll let you get back to the news, I've told you all I had to say."

"Oh, it's over now," his father said crossly.

"Tell you what Dad, try Al Jazeera, it might broaden your horizons."

In that moment Henry felt he didn't care if he never spoke to his parents again, they were poles apart.

A local radio interviewer was followed by a presenter from the regional TV station with a cameraman who panned around the horizon from the top of the Tump, emphasizing the remote location of the farm. Not to be outdone, the rival station arrived unannounced. Henry and Marie had agreed on a simplified version of the story; they had been attracted to buy the farm because they felt it was in a very special setting. They had subsequently heard stories that the spring which fed the farm had healing properties but had no evidence of that, and now they had found the rock carving which expert opinion, (unspecified), had identified as the ancient horned god Cernunnos, the Lord of the Wilds. They thought the find was significant now in view of growing awareness of the loss of natural habitat and the destruction of the environment.

Everyone wanted to interview Jack as the boy who had made the discovery but he said very little, so apart from showing his picture it was left to his parents to do the talking. When the story went out on radio and TV there was interest from national papers as well as the local press and it was several days before they were able to shut the front door and retreat into the kitchen without being interrupted.

The publicity had the desired effect however and

people came to see the carving and stayed to buy crafts and have cream teas.

Henry had the satisfaction of a call from his father asking for any details the media had missed. His friends assumed he had private information and for some reason he found he had nothing to add to what they had already heard; in fact he had been forced to resort to iPlayer to be able to discuss the matter at all. He seemed to be blaming Henry for leaving him in the dark.

"You might have let us know instead of leaving us to look like fools when our own son is being interviewed all over the place. Really Henry, you have no consideration for us, we are your parents after all."

He also had a call from one of the partners at his old firm; he had taken a month's salary in lieu of notice so was now no longer an employee.

"Well, you're a dark horse Henry," he said. "I guess this discovery could make your fortune with all the publicity it's getting if it's properly exploited. Now what I'd like to propose is that we handle it for you. I don't have to tell you that having a prestigious company name behind the promotion will give it added value and handled correctly it will be too big for a one man band. I'm thinking a documentary with foreign rights to start with, I have some contacts I can call on, now what do you say?"

"Thank you for your interest, but I don't think our vision of the way forward agrees with your approach."

Nice to have the upper hand for once.

"Let's not be too hasty about this, Henry, I'm sure there's a lot we can discuss. You know we are always flexible and open to the client's opinion."

"I'm afraid you will have to accept my decision as final, our own plans are in train, but thank you for calling."

A few more pleasantries and that was the end of his association with his old life, and it felt good.

There were similar calls in a different vein from various academic bodies wanting to fund archaeological digs around the Tump. Henry and Marie had no intention of letting anyone disturb the site and were not even prepared to allow a geophysical survey.

"I don't want  anyone poking about the Tump or sending electrical probes into it or whatever  they want to do." Jack was upset at the thought of any interference.

"Don't worry," Marie told him, "We won't allow any investigations. That's not what it's about for us either. People can come and look at the carving if they treat it with respect but we don't want anyone disturbing it."

Marie was surprised to see Sally drive into the yard by herself and as the Fiesta turned round she saw that the 'L' plates were missing.

"You passed your test? You didn't tell me you were taking it."

"I didn't want people to know in case I failed, but I had a few proper lessons and went for it."

"So now you're driving around the countryside celebrating I suppose!"

"Well no, I have a reason to call. I have something to tell you."

"Let's get the kettle on then, have a seat. So what's the

great news?"

"We're getting married. Josh asked me that evening while we were looking at the carving we don't see any reason to hang about. It's either now or wait 'til the Spring between lambing and calving, you know what it's like."

"So when is the big day and how are you doing it?" Marie was pleased if a little surprised.

"We've got it all sorted; it's a simple country wedding though we'll end up with a lot of people I guess. It's the last Saturday in September at the church and then next door to the village hall for the reception. I didn't realise what a nice space that was, they got special funding for community halls a few years ago and it's lovely inside with a full kitchen. The Plough are doing the bar and a good buffet but I'll do some cooking myself and Mrs. Headley from the bakers has a sister who does celebration cakes. Hannah is making my dress and a silk waistcoat for Josh, so really we're sorted. I wondered if Chloe would like to be a bridesmaid?"

"Oh, she'll love that, you can ask her yourself, she'll be over the moon. Thank you Sally. So who's coming? Your mother and brother?"

"Yes, one of the cottages is free so that works out well; Mum's met Josh, she came down for a few days in June, although this wasn't on the cards then. Apart from that, just a few of my uni friends, I haven't kept in touch with many of them given what was going on before. Then there's you, and I'm going to talk Lilian into coming, the gang from the Hall, and half the village on Josh's side of course. A couple of people from the folk club are in a ceilidh band, so that's the music sorted."

"Is your father coming over?"

"No, but we're going to Switzerland for the honeymoon. Dad is paying for the flights and car hire and a family runs a hotel in Interlaken. The weather should be warm in October and we can go down to the Italian border and the lakes if we feel like it. We'll stay a couple of nights with Dad and Katrin in Zurich before we fly home."

"You seem to have everything covered, congratulations!"

Marie hugged her, thinking how quickly her life had turned around and how right this seemed.

The new school term started and Jack had to travel quite a distance on the bus every day. He had his friends from the village for company and although he said behaviour on the journey was rowdy sometimes, he soon settled into the routine. Marie and Henry were surprised that he seemed so little bothered by the increased number of visitors to the farm and all the attention focused on the Tump. It was as if he was detached from the carving now, which was a relief because they had feared during the summer that he was getting obsessed by it.

One weekend Henry broached the subject, asking,

"Are you not finding it too much having so many people coming to look at the carving? It's calming down now the media have moved on and I'm sure there's bound to be a lull over the winter."

"It's OK, Dad," Jack assured him, "It's doing what we needed isn't it? More sales for the gallery and they all go away before evening so it's peaceful again then, and they aren't disturbing the wildlife, they keep to the path."

"So long as you're alright with it, that's all that

matters."

Henry was pleased to see his son playing football and spending time with his friends, it seemed they needn't have worried.

Jack went up to see Lilian later in the morning; he felt he could talk to her better than anyone, she never wanted him to explain and always had something to add. There was smoke coming from her chimney and the van door was open as usual but she was nowhere to be seen, so he settled on the step with Taffy, now obviously pregnant, to wait. After a while he saw her coming back up the track from the village carrying an old holdall with her shopping.

"I don't know why I left it 'til Saturday to go down there, it's heaving with grockles, and quite a few round at your place too."

"I know," he replied, "That's why I came up here, and to see you of course."

They had developed an easy relationship which Lilian had come to treasure, but she reminded herself that as Jack grew older he would have more exciting things to do than visit an old woman.

"How are you feeling about your discovery now? Do you sometimes wish you'd left well alone?"

"Oh No, we have to make a living and this seems to be doing the trick. Mum and Dad are happy to deal with that side of it and Chloe really likes the people coming."

"And what about you?"

"Nothing has changed for me. I still hear the music at night and sometimes the figure appears on the Tump, and there's still the power in the landscape, don't you feel that too?"

"Oh yes, but I'm out of it up here. I think the power is everywhere, not just here, although it's stronger here of course. That's probably why people long to come out into the countryside, the power in Nature feeds the soul doesn't it? I think it must be everywhere though, even in the city if you look for it; it's muted if the earth is buried under concrete but it's in every blade of grass on a bit of wasteland, in every tiny plant that struggles up between the paving stones and of course in parks and people's gardens, though the more those spaces are managed, the less the force of nature can express itself. Wild things creep in everywhere though, urban foxes, rats, seagulls and pigeons in the city and garden birds."

"But there's too much interference isn't there?" Jack complained, "Fewer places for wild things to live and too much pollution."

"Yes, but people are becoming more aware of that aren't they? And the carving is doing a good job at spreading the word. It's a kind of ambassador for Nature."

"You're right, it's gone viral, everyone is talking about it online, people are using the image," Jack told her. " Jed is making copies in metal and they are selling like mad in the gallery, and Dad's looking into having some tee shirts made and sweat shirts with the logo. They've patented it."

"Very wise of them, but don't you mind seeing it used like that?"

"No I don't because I've realised something. The Cernunnos itself is only some ancient people's idea of how the power in the landscape looks, but that isn't it.

259

You can't contain it like that, it's free and it can take any form it likes. We're part of Nature too, human beings can be part of it, interpreting it if you like. We're witnesses. "

"Is that how you see yourself, young Jack?" she asked fondly.   Lilian was struck again by his unique viewpoint.

"I'm still watching and learning that's all. Maybe one day I'll need to do something about it."

"I'm sure when you find out what that is, a great many people will listen," she told him.

Taffy was turning round and round in her bed, churning up the extra blanket Marie had put in for her.

"She's really restless now, I think it could be today," she said at breakfast.

'That was a mistake,' she thought, as instantly Chloe and Jack resisted going to school, they wanted to stay to see the puppies born.

"It could take ages," Marie told them, though looking at the bitch she didn't believe it, "It might not happen 'til this evening," and chivvied  them out of the door.

Both Marie and Henry were more anxious than they liked to admit; a healthy young bitch should surely be able to whelp on her own but they loved Taffy and neither of them had any experience with this.

"Shall we call Ellie do you think?" Henry asked as they met in the kitchen again, each drawn back in to check whether labour had begun.

" We can't expect her to spend all day here, and we could be wrong, it might be too early. We can call her later if we're worried," Marie replied.

At midday there was definitely something going on

and very soon the first tiny blind puppy appeared, followed at intervals by five more. Taffy licked them dry in turn, and soon she was lying on her side while they suckled in a row, each plugged in to a swollen nipple. Henry and Marie laughed to see them, so small with their snubbed faces, hardly looking like puppies at all. It was  warm by the Aga and they made sure the basket was away from any draught; apart from praising Taffy and stroking her gently which made her wag her tail lazily, there was little left for the humans to do.

Marie called Josh to tell him that Merle was a father, although he had sired many litters before, usually by arrangement and on the understanding that Josh would have the pick of the litter in return. Since this was an accident, he had the grace not to ask, but Henry and Marie agreed they should offer him one, though maybe they would let the children choose which one to keep for themselves first. It seemed only fair as they were hoping Josh would help to find buyers for the others in due course.

When the children came home they were ecstatic, but they knew enough about animals now not to crowd the basket or touch the puppies yet, leaving them in peace to suckle and sleep. It was a while before Taffy left the basket, first going outside briefly and then drinking from her water bowl. She didn't seem hungry but by next morning her plate was empty and she seemed to have got over the novel experience of giving birth and was already a devoted mother.

# Chapter 18

The wedding day dawned sunny and warm with the promise of perfect late summer weather. Marie had invited Sally to stay over at Holtbourne in the tradition that the groom should not see the bride until they met at the altar, but she and Josh refused to be separated for the night. She did pack him off to Thomas's house across the courtyard to dress however, leaving her to get ready with Hannah and Marie as maids of honour and a very excited Chloe in her new bridesmaid's frock.

There had been several dress fittings but Hannah was anxious until she saw the effect with heels and a circlet of white rose buds and 'baby's breath' in Sally's glorious chestnut hair; she had never had such a vital commission before. There was much discussion about putting Sally's hair up, but the consensus was that it would be a shame to hide it. They compromised by brushing her hair off her forehead, secured with a silver hair slide which was Sophie's gift, to reveal the heart shaped neckline and shoulder detail of the ivory dress and let her riotous mass of curls fall loose down her back.

Thomas had joked about taking Josh to the church in the small tractor decked with white ribbons but no-one took it seriously until he drove it round to the house door, hosed down and as clean as he could make it. Sally's brother Paul was more conventional, driving her to church to arrive just a few minutes late when everyone was settled in the pews and full of expectation.

Sally's friends from Mennad had used all their artistic skill to decorate the village hall and church and as the organ began the wedding march the scene was set for her entrance on Paul's arm, followed by Chloe with Marie and Hannah.

Turning to watch her progress up the aisle, Josh knew he would remember this moment for the rest of his life. He had never seen her so radiant and his heart swelled with joy and pride. Thomas grinned widely at him, nodding his approval; his brother had got himself a truly beautiful bride. Sally's mother was not the only one to wipe away a tear as they exchanged vows and the rings which Sophie had made were placed on their fingers.

The public kiss was deliberately restrained but as they left the church in a shower of rose petals and walked round to the village hall there was a growing buzz of excited talk and everyone unwound, prepared to enjoy a relaxed celebration for the rest of the day. There was plenty to eat and drink and no speeches, just a toast when the cake was cut. Josh took off his formal grey jacket to reveal the bright patterned silk waistcoat Hannah had made and that was a signal for the ceilidh to begin.

Lilian, who surprised everyone by appearing in a long skirt and satin blouse, slipped away, soon followed by George who had sampled most of the food and drunk enough good beer for one evening. The guests danced, or sat about at tables chatting while Jack, Ryan and Sean perched on the steps outside with some bottles of beer they had filched from under the bar. They were soon joined by other village boys and larked about having a party of their own.

Thomas and Ellie were sitting in a corner surveying the scene.

"That went off well," Thomas said. "My brother's done alright for himself I reckon."

"I hope you're not mistaken, they haven't known each other five minutes," Ellie replied sourly; she had had a few drinks and it loosened her tongue.

"You really don't like her do you?" This was a realisation for Thomas. "What have you got against her?"

"Nothing personal, it's just a risk that's all. If it doesn't work out she could have a claim on the farm, and if they have kids it'll spoil Ryan and Sean's inheritance. Have you not thought of that? "

"Is that what's been getting at you all this time? You'd rather Josh was lonely all his life so our boys can inherit his share is that it?"

"He wasn't lonely, he was never serious about anyone 'til he met Sally. I just wish it had stayed that way."

Thomas turned to look at his wife and didn't like what he saw in her face.

"I don't want you bringing this up again. He's my brother and he's entitled to do what he likes with his share of the farm. We're a family and holding together is what counts in good times and bad. Sally is part of that now and if they have children I for one will be glad. Now let's have no more of this ill-feeling, you need to get over it for everyone's sake."

He went to get another drink, feeling the merriment drain away like water, sobering him up so that when he found Josh saying goodnight to some revellers who were

264

leaving, his manner was serious when he shook his hand and said,

" Congratulations Bro, I just want you to know I'm here for both of you. Sally's a lovely girl, I wish you every happiness."

"Thank you Thomas," Josh was puzzled by his manner but he put it down to the drink talking. "I really appreciate that, we're a good team aren't we, us and the girls, and your boys too. This family's come through some hard times, but we always pull together."

They embraced then in an awkward bear hug and Thomas withdrew, having shown more emotion than he was comfortable with.

It was a still starlit night when Josh and Sally were at last alone, standing outside their own front door. Josh produced the key,saying,

"I've never used this door before, so here we go, a new beginning."

He picked her up, feeling the smooth cool fabric of her skirt under his palms,and careful not to step on the trailing hem, he kicked the door closed behind him and carried her upstairs. The room was more welcoming than the first time he had brought her to his bed, lived in now, with decorative personal items, but their sense of wonder was the same. Their bodies were attuned now and their union even deeper and more satisfying so that when at last they slept they were encircled by an unbreakable bond of love strong enough to last their whole lives through.

The year turned and it was early autumn again. The stags

began to bolve up on the moor and Marie decided to put Basil in with the ewes a few weeks early so that she would have finished lambing before next Easter when they were confident that the gallery would be busy. They separated the well- grown ewe lambs they had kept back from market since they were not ready to mate this year; next season they would have to find another ram to serve Basil's daughters.

Standing at his window in the dark, Jack was aware that the music had changed and the atmosphere was charged with a different, more urgent vibration. He could hear the low notes of Cernunnos's horn again and he felt a deep connection to the changing season, excited and energized, yet at peace within himself. For Jack there was no conflict between his boyhood lived in the exterior world and his identification with the power in the landscape, both were his true nature and he didn't need to speculate how they would come together in the future.

Trees resplendent in red and gold and warm damp days smelling of wet leaves gave way to frosty mornings and cold nights. The farmers moved their stock indoors or onto sheltered pasture, cleared ditches and trimmed hedges, preparing for the short winter days ahead.

At Holtbourne the gallery was still busy with people buying Christmas presents and stopping to eat mince pies and drink mulled wine, alcohol free since they didn't have a drinks licence. Henry cleared the poly tunnels except for the exotic plants which he moved to one end which he insulated with bubble plastic to keep them frost free. He did his best to secure the structures against winter gales,erecting wind breaks to protect them from the prevailing Westerlies. The kitchen garden was still producing well and some of the vegetables could be stored for the winter.

Marie was cooking for Christmas and making sure the freezers were well stocked in case they got snowed in; they had been lucky last year but Exmoor weather is unpredictable.

On Christmas Eve Sally and Josh were wrapping the last presents to take over to the farm house next morning.

"Do you mind having Christmas lunch on our own here?" Sally asked. "We could have gone to Thomas and Ellie if you wanted."

She felt a bit guilty that she had encouraged him to break that tradition but she was sure Ellie didn't really want them there all day.

"No, it's lovely to have our first Christmas in our own home. We've got the tree and a roaring fire, it's very festive, and anyway we're going over to Holtbourne on boxing day. There, that's done, I'll open a bottle of wine."

"Not for me thanks, I'll stick with the juice."

"Are you sure? OK, perhaps I'll just have a beer then."

He came back from the kitchen and settled on the sofa, holding out his hand for her to join him, drawing her down to sit on his knee. She rested her head against her favourite place on his shoulder.

"Ah, this is good isn't it?" he said. "So peaceful, just the fire crackling."

"Actually this might be the last really peaceful Christmas we get," she told him.

"So, who are you thinking of inviting next year?" he wanted to know.

"I think you and I have managed to invite a new little person into our lives for next Christmas." She sat up to gauge his expression.

"Good lord, you mean?" Instinctively his hand moved to cover her flat stomach. "Are you certain ?"

"I've done the test, but I wasn't sure you'd be pleased."

"I'm delighted, it's amazing, fantastic."

He was hugging her and showering her face with kisses. He could process it later, but he knew his immediate reaction now would affect her deeply.

"I know you had doubts about being a father, we should have talked about it more but it seemed like early days."

"That's all in the past, loving you has changed how I feel about myself and anyway, I'm a farmer, breeding is what we do, in all its forms. We have a home and security to offer this child and plenty of love to give, being a family is what it's all about isn't it? What a Christmas present, I can't wait to tell Thomas."

'I know one person who won't be pleased,' thought Sally, but she wasn't going to let it spoil her joy.

It was a family Christmas at Holtbourne too; George was coming over for lunch and they had persuaded Lilian to join them. On Christmas Eve, Henry and Marie were sitting in front of the fire with the children and everyone had at least one puppy on their lap.

"I think Uncle George and Dr. Laidlaw should marry each other, then they wouldn't be lonely," Chloe suggested.

Henry nearly choked on his wine, laughing.

"Promise me you won't say that to either of them, they'd both run a mile in opposite directions," he told her. "Are we all set for the boxing day bash then?"

"Yes, I make it about twenty of us all told including some of the crafters. I told everyone to come about twelve. It's a pity Maggs couldn't get down for New Year, what did you say she was doing?"

"She's going to Italy with a friend, his wife has thrown him out apparently."

"That sounds messy, I hope she doesn't get too involved."

"Oh, Maggs can take care of herself." He hoped he was right, but he said no more, it wasn't for him to break a confidence.

"Right kids, you've hung your stockings up on the mantel and put out the mince pies and sherry for Santa. Can you get the reindeers' carrots Chloe? They're on the draining board."

Henry was enjoying this almost more than the children, in fact Jack was getting quite sniffy about the whole ritual.

"Don't spoil it for Chloe," Marie cautioned him while she was out of the room.

"For Heaven's sake, she doesn't believe in it either, not really," he said in a stage whisper.

"Well I do,"Henry said decisively, "So please take that look off your face."

"Sorry Dad, it's just a bit childish."

"Life's serious enough son, let us old grown ups have a little fun."

Jack rolled his eyes but he helped Chloe arrange the carrots on the hearth.

"Right, off to bed with you then, and if you get up at stupid o'clock you can open your stockings but you're old enough now to keep quiet 'til at least seven thirty, understood?" Henry was hoping for a bit of a lie in.

They hugged the children.

"Be up in a minute to tuck you in,"Marie told them.

Henry opened the door of the log burner and poured them another glass of wine as Marie came back downstairs. A lamp glowed in the corner and the cosy room was full of shadows from the fire. They looked at the greenery gathered from around the farm; ivy, holly red with berries and the fir tree with presents piled underneath, and felt a shared sense of achievement and contentment.

"There are three generations of decorations on that tree. Those glass bells were my grandmother's," Marie said.

"Yes, continuity is important isn't it, all those connections," Henry agreed. " And now we have something tangible to hand down to our children, we can keep the farm for our time and pass  it on to them, whatever they choose to do with it."

"I can't see Jack ever leaving this land," Marie said, " And with Chloe's interest in horses, well, they may take over from the sheep in time."

"We can't speculate that far into the future, but our way ahead is clearer than it was last year. We need a proper tea room, we can attach it to the side of the gallery, a wooden building will do."

Henry was drawing up plans in his head. Marie was still

taking stock.

"What a year this has been, such a roller coaster. We really were in over our heads. Looking back, it was crazy coming here, what were we thinking? But then we had this amazing stroke of luck. Maybe we were meant to be here after all, it does feel that way."

"If we are custodians of the land, I think this farm is in good hands, now and in the years to come. There's one ancient custom I'm all for at least," he told her.

"What's that?"

"Come here and I'll show you." Henry kissed her under the mistletoe, saying, "I wonder how many lovers have done that in this room?"

The End

Also by Rita Hesmond from Amazon

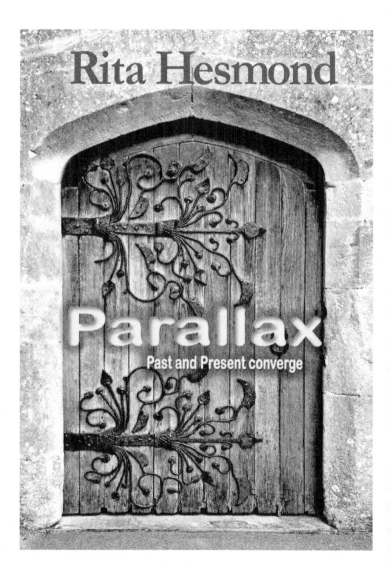

Rita Hesmond

**Parallax**

Past and Present converge

Printed in Great Britain
by Amazon